Claiming Canaan: Milcah's Journey

Barbara M. Britton

May you go forth with God like the daughters of Zelophehad.

Blessings,

Barbara

Claiming Canaan: Milcah's Journey
COPYRIGHT 2020 by Barbara M. Britton

Contact Information: titleadmin@pelicanbookgroup.com

All scripture quotations, unless otherwise indicated, are taken from the Holy Bible, New International Version(R), NIV(R), Copyright 1973, 1978, 1984, 2011 by Biblica, Inc.™ Used by permission of Zondervan. All rights reserved worldwide.
www.zondervan.com

Cover Art by *Nicola Martinez*

Harbourlight Books, a division of Pelican Ventures, LLC
www.pelicanbookgroup.com PO Box 1738 *Aztec, NM * 87410

Harbourlight Books sail and mast logo is a trademark of Pelican Ventures, LLC

Publishing History
First Harbourlight Edition, 2020
Paperback Edition ISBN 978-1-5223-0254-4
SE Paperback Edition ISBN 978-1-5223-0295-7
Electronic Edition ISBN 978-1-5223-0250-6
Published in the United States of America

Dedication

To all the men and women who go forth with God.

Acknowledgements

This book would not have been possible without the help of so many people. My family has been the best cheering section throughout my publishing career. I am blessed to have their love, encouragement, and support.

A big thank you goes to my editor, Fay Lamb, who helped make the daughters of Zelophehad shine again. I am also blessed to have Nicola Martinez in my publishing corner. She has brought all my stories to light through her leadership at Pelican Book Group.

My critique partner Betsy Norman always makes me a better writer. Our Brainstorming group encourages me weekly. Thank you: Jill Bevers, Denise Cychosz, Sandy Goldsworthy, Molly Maka, Karen Miller, Sandee Turriff, and Christine Welman.

A big shout out to Sarah Duncan Sundquist and Molly Duncan for sharing their animal stories with me. Noah's sling and nest came from Sarah and Molly's livestock adventures.

The author communities of WisRWA, ACFW, RWA, SCBWI, and Pelican Book Group, have been a huge support in my writing career.

My church family has kept me going during good times and bad. What a blessing to have their loving support.

And last, but not least, The Lord God Almighty, for giving me the gift of creativity and breath each day to write these stories. I am a cancer survivor, and not a day goes by that I don't praise the Lord for his healing. To God be the glory.

The Daughters of Zelophehad

Mahlah
Noah
Hoglah
Milcah
Tirzah

The Tribes of Israel from Numbers 26:

Reuben
Simeon
Gad
Judah
Issachar
Zebulun
Manasseh, firstborn of Joseph
Ephraim, son of Joseph
Benjamin
Dan
Asher
Naphtali
Levi, no inheritance of land

Books by Barbara M. Britton

Tribes of Israel Series

Providence: Hannah's Journey
Building Benjamin: Naomi's Journey
Jerusalem Rising: Adah's Journey

Daughters of Zelophehad

Lioness: Mahlah's Journey
Heavenly Lights: Noah's Journey
Claiming Canaan: Milcah's Journey

Prologue

Six years after the battle for Ai
The camp at Gilgal, outside the fallen fortress of Jericho

Milcah *bat* Zelophehad stood in the noonday sun, on a hill not far from the rowed tent tops of camp. She waited with her older sisters. Her sisters waited for their husbands. She waited for Hanoch, the man who had asked her eldest sister if he could arrange a betrothal when he returned from battle. Hanoch, a brave soul, did not care that another suitor lay buried deep beneath the ground somewhere in Canaan.

Battle-hardened warriors traipsed along the path toward their homes in Gilgal. Men from the tribes of Israel, the sons of Jacob, carried satchels of spoils. Some bulging. Others thin. But all contained wealth from fallen cities.

"Do you see them?" she asked, rising on tiptoe. She twisted the gold band on her finger—the ring with the ruby as solid and handsome as her Hanoch. He had sneaked it to her before he departed.

"Not yet," her sister Hoglah said. "I have seen few of our tribesmen. Perhaps the men of Manasseh ventured farther north with Joshua."

Two men passed on the trail. One fighter tugged a wide-bellied cow toward its new home. Would Hanoch bring her livestock?

Her eldest sister's brow furrowed. "Reuben assured me our clansmen would return before spring. Our men may be burdened with carts or taking care of any wounded," Mahlah said.

Hurry beloved. Milcah fisted her hand. Her golden band fit snug against her skin. She would not leave her sundrenched outpost until Hanoch marched toward her eldest sister, bowed, and settled on a time to discuss a marriage feast. *Please, God. May Hanoch make haste.*

Drawing closer, Mahlah wrapped her arm around Milcah's waist. The softness of her sister's veil and the slight scent of myrtle bolstered Milcah's weary bones.

Until.

Until she glimpsed Mahlah's husband, Reuben, stalking closer alongside men from their clan and alongside Hoglah's husband.

She strained her neck. Where was Hanoch? He should be with his clansmen.

Reuben's firm-set mouth and pity-filled eyes impaled her hopeful spirit.

Her vision blurred so that all the men of Manasseh were buoyed by a sea of tears.

"No. It cannot be." She swallowed the last of her whisper.

The shake of Reuben's head revealed her fate.

She slumped in the dirt and wailed.

Death had claimed another intended.

1

*So Joshua took the entire land, just as the Lord had directed
Moses, and he gave it as an inheritance to Israel according to
their tribal divisions. Then the land had rest from war.*
Joshua 11:23

One year later
The Israelite camp at Gilgal in the conquered land of Canaan

Milcah braced her legs on either side of the tent peg,
wrapped a cloth around the tip, and wiggled, jiggled, and
wiggled the peg some more. After almost seven years of
being staked in the same place, the peg battled to stay in
the ground. On this day she would leave Gilgal and leave
the sad memories of lost loves behind.

She dropped her weight and struggled to free the
bronze anchor anew. With a fierce tug, the stake escaped
from its soil home. Taut ramskin buckled as the once-tall
tent sagged to the side.

A squeal emerged from within the cock-eyed
dwelling.

Tirzah, Milcah's youngest sister, poked her head from the tent flap. Her lips crumpled downward like their home.

"What are you doing? I'm hardly dressed." Tirzah's gaze darted down the main pathway. "Enid isn't about? Is he?"

Milcah flung the hand-saving rag over her shoulder. "Your betrothed is in the fields where I am going to fetch a cart and a donkey. We don't want to carry this tent on our own." She quirked a brow at her prune-nosed sister. "Do we?"

Tirzah arched her back. "Truly, not." She covered a yawn. "Will you see if Hoglah has bread baked?"

"Hah. Waking you was trouble enough. Demanding food from Hoglah will make a balking donkey seem tame."

"There may be bread leftover in my pouch," Tirzah said.

"The one with the rocks?" Milcah's mouthed soured. "I'm sure our sister has prepared food for our travels. I'll see what hasn't been packed." Milcah grabbed a coil of rope. "And you have our belongings ready to move. I'd rather donkeys and camels carry the weight and not our shoulders."

As she turned to leave, she thought she saw a tongue returning to Tirzah's mouth. She may have been mistaken. Dawn did not cast much light.

"*Shalom,* Sister." Milcah stifled a laugh. Nothing was going to steal her tempered joy this morn. Year after year of battles had come to an end. No more men would die by the sword. And she and her sisters would claim a portion of the conquered land in their father's name. The name of Zelophehad would live again through his daughters' inheritance.

Whoosh.

A few yards from the trodden path, a tent flattened in the shadowy sunlight. The tribes of Israel would soon be on a march to Shiloh to set up the Tabernacle, the home of the God of Abraham, Isaac, and Jacob. Afterward, her people would not congregate in a camp as one people. The tribes of Israel would separate and settle the land God had bestowed on each son of Jacob.

Milcah headed into the outskirts where her sisters Noah and Hoglah cared for livestock with their husbands. Farther and farther, her sisters had settled to keep up with their growing herds. Bounty was a blessing, but the memory of five dark-haired girls sharing the same tent still nestled in her heart.

Her mother and father had prepared their offspring well for this journey. A heaviness settled behind her eyes. If only her parents had lived to see this day. Mahlah had become a strong leader. Noah oversaw abundant livestock. Hoglah prepared the tastiest of food. All three daughters had married within their father's clan. The clan of Hepher. Her sisters had done as God commanded. Their tribe of Manasseh wouldn't lose a single portion of land. Now, Tirzah was set to marry. Milcah had taken care of their youngest sister all her life. A tear dripped from Milcah's lashes. When Tirzah slept in Enid's tent, what would be left for the fourth daughter of Zelophehad? What did a woman without a husband do as she aged? Those thoughts were best left for another day.

The murmur of excited voices, the squeak of rolling carts, and the clank of clay jars banished the usual silence of early morning.

Dodging a wagon in her path, she cut between staked tents whose owners had not begun their labors. The ground dipped. A pebble lodged between her toes.

Ugh. Not now. She had too many nieces, nephews, and sisters to organize for their journey north.

She grasped the lip of a cleansing jar, bent, and tried to free the small stone making its presence known by poking her fattest toe.

"Why are you dismayed?" a man asked.

Jerking upright, she glanced for the speaker. She was alone in the small alley.

"Isn't your brother married to one of Zelophehad's daughters?"

The questions came from inside the upright tent. Who was inquiring about her sisters?

A laborer in the distance glanced her direction, and she took off her sandal and jiggled the leather all the while listening to the veiled voices. Surely, the neighbor rolling ramskin would see and understand her distress as she balanced on one foot.

"My brother would never listen to reason," a gossiper rasped.

"Your brother cannot hear anything. He's a mute."

Chuckling carried through the tent wall.

Ahh. She knew the identity of one of the men in the tent. Her teeth clenched at the thought of Keenan. The troublemaker had tried to trick her sister Noah into marrying him. Praise God, Keenan's scheme had not succeeded. Though, the menace was now her sister's brother-in-law.

"I am well aware of my brother's curse." Keenan's final word hissed through the tent wall. "My brother will oversee the land of his wife, but two of the daughters of Zelophehad are unmarried. Why should unwed women be allotted land they did not fight for?"

Because God gave us our father's land.

She forced her sandal onto her foot and shuffled

forward with a feigned limp.

Why was Keenan bringing up her inheritance now? Seven years ago, she and her sisters sought out Moses and asked to inherit their deceased father's land. God honored their request, and Moses proclaimed God's ruling to an assembly of elders. Did Keenan mean to question God?

"Moses gave them their father's portion. Do you mean to question his judgment?" Another man's voice echoed Milcah's silent question.

Toda raba. Someone awakened with sense.

"Joshua is the one who conquered Canaan," Keenan argued. "He should limit the girl's allotment. How much land can these women possibly work? The sons of Joseph are a numerous people and our given land is full of forest. Do you want to clear the hillsides while women settle flatter lands?"

"You will need more elders to agree to your demands if you mean to overturn Moses' decree."

Hushed murmuring blended together into an undecipherable hum. Discerning whether Keenan's case gained supporters was futile. Would these men agree with Keenan's assessment? No one was going to steal her inheritance. Not for lack of a husband. Praise be for a troublesome rock. She had stumbled upon another one of Keenan's devious schemes.

Voices quieted.

The tent flap whipped open.

She lunged forward. Her heart skittered into an all-out gallop. Chin down, she pulled her head covering tight to her face, and hurried out of camp, never chancing a glance at Keenan or his cohorts.

Her first chore this morning would be to warn her sisters of Keenan's plot. She had to gather four sisters and get to Joshua before Keenan persuaded elders from the tribes of Ephraim and Manasseh to question her family's allotment. Her sisters had men to challenge this undoing. She did not have a husband or a betrothed. Truly it was not for a lack of trying, but after two dead suitors, no one had ventured to her sister's tent flap to ask about an arrangement of marriage.

Would Joshua heed Keenan's challenge and limit her land? She would not relinquish one crag or valley of her allotment. Seven years had passed, that was true, but elders from Manasseh and all the tribes of Israel, had heard God's decree through Moses. Whether married, or unmarried, her father's double portion of land was coming to his daughters. Zelophehad's name would be carried into Canaan. She had already started to pack her tent and seek a new life.

Only her wicked kinsman could ruin such a glorious day.

2

After warning Hoglah and Noah about Keenan's latest scheme to snatch her land, Milcah hurried to inform her eldest sister. The people of Israel had made haste in their packing. The camp resembled the inside of her tent when all five sisters were changing robes. Men yelled orders. Tents collapsed. Donkey-drawn carts and oxen-led wagons headed north to Shiloh. Warriors from the tribes of Reuben, Gad, and some Manassites traveled closer to the Jordan River.

Rushing down the wide path toward Mahlah's tent, Milcah's chest tightened. Her home lay flattened. She had told Tirzah to finish the work, but the openness, the sight of nothing where she had lived with her family, cramped her stomach. Tirzah had listened. For once. The daughters of Zelophehad were going forth with God into His Promised Land. The land God had portioned for her father.

Reuben, Mahlah's husband, and Jonah, his son, rolled ramskin with ease. Jericho, the walled fortress that had greeted her people, lay ruined, conquered, and burned. The remains of the city were a reminder of the power of the One True God. If God could fell a stone fortress, He could certainly provide a fearless husband for Milcah.

Mahlah carried baby Aaron on her hip while her older children, Amos and Abigail, placed wooden plates and cups into satchels. Working hard as usual, Milcah's sister splayed a blanket on a camel's back with her free hand.

"Good morning, Sister," Mahlah said. "Where is your cart? We must be on our way."

If only packing was their sole worry this day.

"We can pack later. We must seek our leader, for there is another scheme about." Milcah brushed the sweat from her brow. She had raced home like a king's messenger. "Noah and Hoglah will arrive soon with a cart."

"Scheme? What scheme?" Mahlah shifted Aaron on her hip. "Joshua will be supervising the Tabernacle servants. The Ark of our God is being moved to Shiloh. Our leader is not judging petitions."

"Not yet." Milcah bent at the waist and breathed deep. "But soon Joshua's plans will be interrupted by elders from our tribe and others. Keenan is plotting to steal some of our land. I heard him trying to gather supporters when I left camp."

"This is madness." Mahlah's features grew serious. "God bestowed our inheritance. The matter is settled."

"Is anything settled when Keenan is involved?" Contentment never found her kinsman. "He is persuaded that since Tirzah and I do not have husbands, our land should be given to our clansmen."

Reuben stomped closer. A mallet dangled from his hand. "If my wife and sister-in-law are talking about Keenan *ben* Abishua, I know no good can come of it."

"I heard him with my own ears." Milcah leaned forward and tickled her nephew's cheek. "He is challenging some of our inheritance because Tirzah and I have no husbands."

"Nonsense." Reuben rubbed his bearded jaw. "Tirzah is betrothed."

Milcah's spirit heard her brother-in-law's unspoken worry. She was not betrothed. Though, hadn't she been doing what her parents would have wanted? Taking care of her youngest sister, an orphan no less? Her older sisters had families and husbands to attend. Even at nineteen, she could still find someone in due time. Now that war had ebbed, perhaps men interested in her hand would not be concerned about dying in battle.

"Keenan has no right to challenge the amount of land we receive," Mahlah said.

Her sister's one-armed hug was a balm to Milcah's soul. Even baby Aaron reached to grab Milcah's chin.

"We will go to Joshua and remind him of Moses' proclamation."

"Toda raba, Sister." Milcah lay her head on Mahlah's shoulder and kissed her nephew's inquisitive fingers.

Reuben handed his mallet to Jonah. "I will not allow a kinsman to dishonor my father-in-law's name." He turned toward his eldest son. "Jonah, look after your brother and sister."

Amos jutted his chin. "I can look after myself."

Reuben straightened his robe. "Then you watch over Abigail."

Amos arched his back and complained to the blue sky. His younger sister squealed and hugged her brother tight.

"Must we always have the loudest dwelling in camp?" Hoglah halted her plump donkey and guided the cart nearer the sluggish camel.

Praise be her sisters had gathered, Milcah thought. Who could stand against five wronged women?

"We should pray that Reuben will be as ear-splitting

in Keenan's presence." Noah made no move to dismount from her ride. The sash across her chest bulged from the weight of her infant daughter. "Or I could let Miriam wail in protest. Keenan is fond of strong women." Noah patted her whip and laughed. "Now, who will take the babe while I dismount?"

"Give her to me." Hoglah received Miriam with eagerness.

Milcah breathed a silent prayer that one day Hoglah would hold a child of her own.

Noah slid from her donkey. "That"—Noah pressed her lips together—"brother-in-law of mine will not steal one rock from us. He thought he could lay claim to me and my land years ago. It's time he let loose of the hatred in his heart."

"I don't believe it's only in his heart." Milcah's pronouncement slipped from her mouth.

"Milcah?" Tirzah stifled a laugh as she joined the commotion.

"I meant..." What did she mean? She had spoken her thoughts forcefully out into the open. "If Keenan has been storing ill-will towards us for years, then his whole body is consumed by hatred, not solely his heart."

"All the more reason to petition Joshua in haste." Reuben motioned for Jonah to join his brother and sister.

Jonah frowned before herding his siblings like cattle.

Reuben ushered Milcah and her sisters toward the Tabernacle in the center of camp.

Reuben and Mahlah walked almost side by side. What a formidable, though small, army they made with Hoglah and Noah trudging in their wake. Tirzah scanned the workmen packing tents.

"I wish Enid labored in camp." Tirzah squinted into the outskirts. "He would support our inheritance."

Milcah swept hair from Tirzah's face. "I'm sure he is helping his brother with our livestock in Noah and Hoglah's absence. I know he would come if he could." She encouraged her sister with a confident smile. "Do not worry. No man is coming to speak for me. God has already spoken on our behalf."

"He has, hasn't He." Tirzah strolled on ahead, light of foot.

Milcah's eyes grew moist. The daughters of Zelophehad had followed God's laws and God had set their path's straight through wars and trickery and slander.

Lord, have I not proved myself faithful to my sisters and to you?

Keenan would lament the day he turned a blessing from God into a confrontation.

Up ahead, the elaborate curtain of the Tabernacle had vanished. Only its frame remained. Gone were the scarlet, purple, and indigo designs. Even the holiest tent had been removed. Levites carried the gold covered Ark of her God on poles. Her God would not forsake an orphan He had blessed with an inheritance of land. Even if that orphan did not have a betrothal.

She rushed forward and joined Mahlah, Reuben, and her sisters.

"I can speak to my station," Milcah offered. Man did not number his own days, God did. Hanoch's days had been too few to become her husband.

Reuben's brow furrowed. "There is no need. I am an elder of Manasseh as my father was before me. The leaders of our tribe will listen to my voice."

A group of men marched toward the former Tabernacle opening. Dust clouded the air from their shuffling sandals.

She knew the forward-leaning gait and the tightly wrapped turban of the lead conspirator.

"Reuben," she said, a hitch to her voice, "you'd better prepare your words. Here comes our predator with his pack."

3

As soon as her warning left her lips, Keenan turned her direction and glared down his crooked nose. Her foe didn't hesitate, or slow his march, even in Reuben's presence. Keenan never shied from a fight he thought he could win. But then, neither did her sisters. And finally, on this day, they were setting out to claim God's provision.

Their leader, Joshua son of Nun, had his back to the oncoming parties. Joshua's attention seemed fixed on the move of the Ark of the Covenant. Gold glimmered on the Ark from beneath its curtain drape. Tabernacle servants carried the seat of God with poles. No man dared touch it, or they would perish. Eleazar, the high priest, observed the work from Joshua's side.

"Commander," Keenan shouted to their leader.

Milcah quickened her steps. How clever of Keenan to address Joshua as a fellow warrior. Her clansman may have gone to war alongside Joshua, but Reuben had also fought bravely for their people. Her biggest battle would begin in a breath.

"Fearless leader," she called.

Heads turned at her high-pitched summons. Didn't Joshua serve all of Israel? Men, women, and children?

Joshua and Eleazar turned. Mouths agape, their leaders beheld the oncoming rush of people.

"What is the meaning of this disturbance?" Joshua studied the elders' faces before nodding to Reuben and Mahlah. "Our God is going before us to Shiloh. I do not have time to judge grievances. Is that not the job of your elders?" Joshua's head bobbed toward the men surrounding Keenan.

Eleazar cast a glance at Joshua before returning his focus to the pole bearers.

"Many from our tribe of Manasseh are leaving camp," Keenan said. "We must have a decision made about the lands of our clansman, Zelophehad."

Arms clamped tight across his chest, Reuben closed the gap between them.

She slipped beside her oldest sister.

"They are asking for you to rule on what has already been decided." Reuben emboldened his height with a shrug of his shoulders. "My wife is the eldest daughter of Zelophehad. All of us were present when Moses granted the inheritance of Zelophehad to his daughters." Reuben indicated Eleazar. "Our high priest can testify to Moses' pronouncement."

"I can," Eleazar responded without a flinch or a whirl.

Opening his arms as if in praise to God, Keenan

shifted away from Reuben's frame. "We are not here to challenge God. But one of these girls has not followed God's instruction." Keenan's tongue slithered between his teeth. He pointed in Milcah's direction and grinned.

Her mouth soured and drew taut.

An elder joined Keenan's station. "The girl has not married within the clan of Hepher. Are we to give her land not overseen by a man? Our tribe is numerous, but our people have only received a small allotment."

"Small?" Joshua's forehead puckered like a baked prune. "Clear the forests and foothills. God has been generous bestowing land on the sons of Joseph. We have a portion from Gilgal to the northern mountains." Joshua's voice had gone from understanding judge to battle commander. "Do not insult God's provision."

Eleazar rounded at Joshua's roar. Levites stopped their labors.

Milcah and her sisters stilled. Not even a side-eyed glance was shared.

"Leader." Keenan bowed. "The land for one of the girls is our issue. She has no offer of marriage from a clansman."

Her face flamed. She had been sought out by two suitable men. Was she to question God in their deaths?

She bowed. "I have not given up on marriage." Her hands trembled as she disputed her elders. How dare Keenan claim to know her future or her desires. "God said I could marry whomever I pleased from my father's clan. Two men approached my sister and her husband about a betrothal. My heart pains that they are no longer living."

Her sister stroked her back, but Mahlah's kindness did nothing to douse the blaze in her bones.

An elder flailed his arms. "How can a woman without a husband tend to fields and flocks. Can she fight off the pagans living near our lands?"

"We will not leave our sister alone," Mahlah said with a firm sandal stomp. "We have always cared for one another."

"What do these women know about fighting," Keenan added.

"Enough." Joshua dipped his chin at Keenan and his gaggle of elders. "These women have every right to their father's portion of land. I expect the elders of Manasseh to honor God's word."

Toda raba, Adonai.

Joshua turned his scarlet-cheeked face toward her.

Why did she feel she was not as victorious as she thought?

"It is good for a woman to marry. See that you have a husband by next year's harvest." Joshua stepped closer. "Do not force me to fight more battles with your elders." His voice was secret-sharing low. "Receive a betrothal request and prosper on your land."

"Where would that land be?" Her stomach cramped. It may have been bold to ask, but then pronouncements made by the high priest and Joshua were not easily dismissed. Especially when the elders of her tribe were in attendance. If she was being forced into a certain future, she had a right to know where her future would prosper.

Keenan clapped his hands. "We do not need to trouble our leader with such a task. Other tribes have not received their inheritance."

"Let us end this quarrel." Eleazar slipped a hand behind his golden breastplate. Twelve gems glimmered on the breastplate, one for each of Jacob's sons. Faceted stones sparked in the light as the high priest's hand moved behind the gilded armor. She could have sworn her forefather Joseph's stone sparkled brightest.

Joshua placed his hands together and bowed toward their priest.

Eleazar cleared his throat and withdrew his hands. Whatever he was holding remained shielded behind his ornate breastplate. "Zelophehad's daughters will travel north and settle in the uppermost valley given to the tribe of Manasseh. Between the mountains you will find the land God has bestowed upon your father. Settle in the outskirts of Megiddo." Eleazar dipped his chin. "Be fruitful and uphold the teachings of God."

Everyone bowed. Even Joshua.

"We will do as we are told." Mahlah kept her face to the ground in a show of reverence.

She and her sisters uttered an agreement and rose slowly.

"Praise be to the God of Abraham, Isaac, and Jacob," Milcah said. And oh, how she needed God. What man would seek a marriage with her scandalous reputation? Ask for her hand, and you would be buried in the dirt.

Eleazar nodded her direction and strode after the Levites who had waited with the Ark of the Covenant not far from its collapsed holy home.

Joshua started after Eleazar.

"Commander." Keenan darted after their leader. "Aren't there Canaanites still living in the cities on the other side of the valley. They have chariots. Will women be able to rise up against a vengeful army?"

Joshua grasped his collar and tugged. His face became as red as the threads on Eleazar's embroidered robe. "Did you not hear our high priest? The matter of the land has been settled. Haven't we lived near the graveyard that was Jericho? No Canaanite city can stand against our God." Their leader pointed to the downed tents and packed mules of the camp. "See to your family and your portion.

Our people must leave for Shiloh and establish the house of God."

Reuben thumped a fist to his chest. "I will protect these women and our lands."

And she had no doubt that her brother-in-law would protect her, but could he find her a man that was willing to risk death to become her husband? Had one year removed the belief that to care for her cost a man his life?

Nearby, a Levite's tent slumped to the ground.

Why did her future feel like flat, dusty, ramskin?

4

Milcah rubbed her temples. Her head had ached for over two days. Every footfall on their trip north to Shiloh sent a boom of pain through her temples. Why did she have to think so much? Because the elders had not spoken without merit. How was one woman going to manage lands and entice a husband when everyone believed her to be cursed? *Ask to marry the fourth daughter of Zelophehad and you will die in battle or from infection.* Could she mourn another suitor?

She picked up a basket and left her newly staked tent. The generous moon banished the shadows surrounding her brief home in Shiloh. She sauntered toward Mahlah's tent. In a few days, Milcah would scout her land and then form a plan to catch the attention of a brave clansman.

As she approached the tent, her sister stopped scraping plates near a dying campfire.

"Everyone has eaten," Mahlah said over her shoulder.

"Not your babe." Milcah nodded to where Abigail sat with baby Aaron. His delightful noises were growing louder. "I will gather kindling for the fire while you care for your son."

Before her sister could refuse her offer, Milcah hurried away. Lifting her chin to the darkening sky, she prayed, "Lord, give me wisdom. Provide a husband for me within a year, or sooner."

Her chest ached with pressed-down affection for Hanoch. Memories of her former love filled her mind. Remembering his deep-dimpled, confident smile brought tears to her eyes. She sniffled and willed herself to be strong.

"Be strong and courageous." Isn't that what Joshua commanded her people to be?

She slowed her steps and searched for a piece of starry sky not blocked by branches.

"I don't know if I can care for another man, Lord, but You can change my heart. May You open it straightaway to a respectable clansman."

The name of her father deserved to be carried into the Promised Land. Not just by four daughters, but by all five. Scheming elders would not steal her provision. She would do what Joshua and God had commanded, with or without a husband. She would love the Lord, her God, and serve Him forever.

Her sandal crunched on something solid. She glanced at the dirt. Praise be. A massive oak had scattered twigs and small branches on the ground for her to pluck. Was this bounty a sign that God had heard her prayer? She laughed as she bent to gather the wood. How could twigs be a sign?

Something plunked to the soil by the trunk of the tree.

She flinched and jumped backward.

End over end, a log of a branch traveled closer, resting near her sandal. Trees didn't shed. She glanced into the leafy bush of the oak.

A man squatted on a tree limb.

She screamed. And stumbled. And dropped her basket.

Grabbing the thick log at her feet, she pointed it at the tree lounger.

Was it an enemy? A Canaanite?

"If you move, I will scream and bring all of Israel's warriors down upon you." Her voice grew bolder with each word. Surely, a shepherd would hear her distress?

"Do not call our kin," the man said. His tone cast dispersions on her presence.

Wait.

Only one eye glistened in the shadows. The other eye was patched.

Her chest slumped. She knew this gawker. Eli ben Abishua. In what folly did he partake? And why was he crouched in a tree?

"Eli, I thought you were a Canaanite. What are you doing sitting in that oak?" She huffed her words as her heart and lungs quieted their rampage. She lowered her split-branch weapon. "Are you drunk?"

"If I was, would I be able to climb a tree?" He carefully rose and grasped the branch above his head.

"But you have imbibed?" Her clansman was not known for being sober.

"Earlier perhaps. Now leave me be." He motioned for her to be on her way.

She took a step forward and gathered her basket. A coiled rope swung from Eli's belt. What did her clansman need with a rope? Especially in a tree? Her skin pimpled. Was Eli forlorn? He hadn't been as jovial since his disfigurement. Perhaps if she stalled, someone else would arrive to chastise Eli.

"Why do you have so much rope?" She kept her inquisition calm.

"It's nothing" He repositioned his hold on the high branch.

"Truly, it is. It could come loose and hit me on the head." She didn't need to increase the throbbing in her temples.

"If it does strike you, I won't have to answer so many questions." He cleared his throat. "Move along."

Should she? Eli wasn't known for his wisdom. Hovering above the ground, drunk, and in a tree fit with Eli's reputation. Once, he'd consumed so much wine that he followed tribesmen into a pagan pit of worship. He even brought her sister Hoglah and their cousin with him.

She shivered. Visions of Eli's body, limp and hanging from the wide branch of the oak flashed in her mind. Her feet stayed firmly planted below the branches.

"The only one I know to sling animals from a tree is my sister, Noah. Come down and help me find wood for the fire." Would he listen to her? For once?

He shook his wild head of hair. "At least Noah has livestock and land. What does a third son inherit?"

"Eli, come down." Her heart rhythm thrummed in her ears. Should she run and fetch Reuben? Though, if she left Eli alone, he could knot a noose, jump, and—

"Get down now." She jabbed her basket at his shadowed face.

"I don't have to listen to you squawk." Eli shuffled his feet on the supporting branch and edged farther from the trunk.

Crack!

The branch split in half.

With his support thinned, Eli swung from the high branch, one-handed.

"Hang on," she shouted.

His sandals failed to find another foothold. Eli's free

hand grasped at a nearby branch. Leaves rustled.

"Watch out." Eli's scarred face crumpled in a snarl.

Her clansman bored down upon her.

She screamed and attempted to flee.

Body weight engulfed her, slamming her spine into the ground. Like a lark, her basket flew in the air, taking the breath from her lungs with it.

Warmth swarmed her senses. Her skin was touching Eli's skin. A bristle of a beard scratched her neck. This couldn't be happening.

"Get off me." She tried to shift his body, but he didn't budge. His solid rock of a build triumphed over her spindly arms. Rope weighed heavy on her hip.

Eli moaned. He rolled on his side, easing the pressure off of her chest. Bracing an arm on the ground, he struggled to stand. His legs and hers battled to see who could gain a foothold. He won. Her limbs refused to rush. She attempted to rise, but she would have sworn leaves twirled and swirled inside her head. Perhaps lying flat was best.

"Milcah?" Mahlah's shriek soared to the stars.

"Eli. What are you doing? You've—you've." Mahlah grasped her sister's arm and drug her farther from their clansman. "You've touched my sister."

"I fell out of a tree," he said, his response weak.

More like slammed me into a fortress wall. Milcah's tongue tasted salt and soil. Saliva pooled in her mouth as she sat, slumped on the ground.

Reuben and Jonah sprinted toward Eli. Reuben grasped the tree dweller's collar and twisted.

With her lip swelling, she whispered to Mahlah, "I believe he wanted to die."

"He may get his chance." Mahlah ran a hand over Milcah's legs. "If he doesn't offer to marry you, Reuben and the elders will stone him for this assault. You are an unwed orphan."

She didn't need the reminder.

5

Milcah paced inside her tent, limping slightly. The tingling on her lip confirmed her dilemma. A man had touched her—all over. The scoundrel was Eli. True, he was a clansman, but he also was a son of Abishua and brother to Keenan. But Eli? Had God answered her prayer swiftly? Was she truly going to be betrothed to a fool? Part of her hoped her curse was true and that Eli would not be her husband. Her conscience squeezed her heart. She couldn't wish death upon anyone, even Eli. If this was God's answer to her petition, then she would make the best of it. Hadn't Joshua warned them to be strong and courageous? She would need every blood drip of strength to be known by Eli.

"You are not at fault, Sister." Mahlah wrung her hands as she sat next to Tirzah on a nearby bed mat. Tirzah tossed a stone from hand to hand as if the conversation did not pertain to her family.

Before Milcah could lament being assaulted by a falling clansman, the tent flap whipped open. Hoglah scrambled into the tent. Noah followed with Miriam cradled on her hip.

"Tell me it isn't true?" Hoglah's words rushed forth. "It's slander of our father's name as always." Hoglah's gaze beheld Mahlah, then Tirzah, then impaled Milcah. "Well, speak."

Milcah turned to Noah who kissed her daughter and then tipped her head as if waiting for an engaging story.

"What did you hear?" Perhaps the gossip wasn't as bad as she presumed.

Noah quirked a brow. With her sandal, she tapped the woven mat that Mahlah and Tirzah shared. "We heard that Eli flattened you like a bed mat."

Tirzah laughed.

"Sister, do not make light of this." Mahlah smoothed Tirzah's loose strands of hair.

"What?" Tirzah shrugged and clutched her stone. "I have been betrothed for a year."

"I am only repeating what is being whispered among our clan," Noah said.

Hoglah stomped closer and inspected Milcah's split lip. "He attacked her. There is still dried blood on her face. What are Reuben and the elders going to do about this?"

Milcah sighed. Was anyone going to listen to her?

"Eli's intent was not to harm me. He toppled out of a tree and knocked me down." Repeating the night's event sounded odd even to her own ears.

"What was he doing in a tree?" Noah gave Mahlah a curious eyebrow raise. "Keenan had to have coaxed him into another plot to seize a portion of our land. Shepherds are lamenting our provision of land in the valley."

Milcah straightened her spine. Fleeting was her pain relief. "Eli had been drinking." Not the best of defenses.

"When doesn't he drink?" Hoglah tickled Miriam's cheek. "I rarely see him sober since his injury."

"Well then, it's easy to see how he lost his balance and

fell from a tree." Milcah rubbed her arms. How was it after returning to the tent, Eli's touch still remained upon her skin?

Hoglah gave a curt laugh. "Because men who have had too much wine always climb unsteady branches instead of falling asleep." She plopped on the mat beside Mahlah. "Eli is a troublemaker. We are all aware of his sins. Abishua and his sons won't rest until they steal some of our land." Hoglah's eyes widened. "Except for Jeremiah. We are all fond of your husband, Noah." She nodded to their sister.

"As am I." Noah grinned. Miriam giggled as if adding to the praise of her father.

Milcah knelt before her sisters stationed on the mat. "I believe Eli meant to do himself harm. He carried a rope onto a high branch."

"Up to no good is all." Hoglah poked Milcah in the chest. "You should be thankful he didn't tie you like a calf."

Tirzah leaned closer to her sisters. "Should we accuse him of more than a fall?"

"No." Her response caused her sisters to draw back. "I will not have Eli's blood on my fingertips. He is a clansman. Everyone would say his death was because of my curse."

Mahlah rubbed her forehead. The grooves resembled deep troughs. "Then you will have a betrothal. It cannot be any other way. His touch was too intimate."

An eerie hum settled in Milcah's ears. If this was a trap, it had played out well. Eli's death would secure her curse. No clansman would seek an arrangement of marriage. If allowed to live, Eli's life would be joined with hers. Until she died. Though, no elder could take her land if she had a husband.

Why did this happen, Lord?

She met Mahlah's teary-eyed gaze. "A betrothal is in order. Our laws have forced my hand. I will honor our father's name and settle his land."

"With Eli?" Hoglah's body trembled. "He almost killed me by leading me into a worship pit for...a false god."

Milcah's mouth parched. Hadn't she worked all of her life to build unity between her sisters? Leave it to Eli to bring dissension with a misguided act. Could she tolerate such a fool? For years? Day after day?

Mahlah grasped Milcah's hand and caressed her skin. She reached out a hand toward Hoglah that went untouched.

"What shall I tell Reuben and the elders?" Mahlah said.

"Tell them..." Milcah blew out one of her last breaths as a woman without a betrothal. "Tell them I will accept an arrangement with Eli, and I will go forth with God."

Hoglah rushed toward the tent flap. "Then you will go forth without me." Before leaving completely, she whirled around. "Eli better stay as far away from me as possible." Hoglah threw the hem of her head covering over her shoulder. "Tell her about the land, Mahlah. I fear it is time."

After casting a stern glance Milcah's direction, Hoglah fled from the tent.

Gone. Her middle sister had abandoned her when she needed the support of her sisters.

Noah kissed Milcah's cheek. Baby Miriam pretended to kiss her cheek as well.

"I will talk to her," Noah said. "She is in shock and remembering past sins that should be left buried." Noah swaddled her babe and hurried out of the tent.

Milcah turned to her eldest sister and Tirzah. "Forgive me." A tear escaped her eye and slid down the side of her face. "All I wanted to do was collect sticks so we could be on our way early in the morning."

Tirzah hugged her with fervor. "There is always the hope that Eli might die before your wedding night."

Milcah cradled Tirzah's plump cheeks in her hands. "We have seen enough of death. And I do not desire to hear any more mutterings about a curse. Let us plan your wedding feast. We will celebrate your union with Enid, and we will celebrate receiving father's portion of the valley."

She glanced at Mahlah. "Now that I have a suitor from father's clan, what has Hoglah done with my land?"

6

A betrothal to Eli was not something Milcah had seen in her future, but taking possession of her father's land had been a blooming vine in her thoughts since the day God bestowed her inheritance. She stiffened at the mention that there might be problems with her portion. With Eli as her husband, she could claim her part of Canaan and remain there until her bones lay buried beneath it. Without him, she had a year until the elders snatched her inheritance. And if Eli didn't offer for her hand, he would be killed, and then she knew no one would seek a betrothal from a woman whose intendeds always died.

"It's my fault." Tirzah's words slurred as she stepped away from Milcah's caress of her cheeks. "I asked Mahlah if my portion of land could join with Hoglah's. Enid and Lamech have been working together overseeing the herds since the battles ended. It would be easier to graze livestock if the brothers had land that joined together." Tirzah pressed her hands flat as if she was going to offer a prayer.

Was that all that Tirzah wanted? A land shift? She would gladly place more distance between Hoglah and Eli.

Milcah nodded. "It makes sense. As we have seen, Hoglah is not fond of my intended."

Placing a hand on Tirzah and Milcah's shoulders, Mahlah leaned into their intimate circle. "I can keep your land in between Hoglah's and Tirzah's if you desire. We all know the past years have been difficult for you." Mahlah gently squeezed Milcah's arm.

Milcah sighed. She did not want to envision Hanoch's handsome features. Not after she had seen Eli's unruly hair and scarred cheekbone. "My days are not going to get easier. It is of little consequence to me where my land is located. As long as I can settle in the valley and carry on my father's name, I will feel blessed."

Tirzah kissed her over and over on her cheek. "Toda raba, Sister. You are welcome to visit my home anytime."

"Even with Eli in tow?" Isolation from her sisters would cause woe to her heart.

"I will show him hospitality." Tirzah cast a glance at their eldest sister.

Their middle sister wouldn't welcome Eli. Already, her clansman was causing her trouble.

Mahlah cleared her throat. "Hoglah will come around. Though, Hoglah's worry will all be for naught if Eli doesn't offer to make arrangements for your marriage. Let us hope Reuben's demands made it through Eli's stupor."

Why did her delight in a wedding celebration always end in mourning? Milcah bit her lip. A stabbing pain seeped to her chin.

"You really believe Eli would choose death over me?"

Tirzah removed the stone she had placed in her satchel and tossed it in the air.

"One can only hope."

"Tirzah!" Mahlah rebuked their youngest sibling.

"Can't we still have some sisterly secrets?" Tirzah

blew out a loud breath. "Let's go find out if Eli is going to join our family."

Mahlah straightened Milcah's robe and head covering. "Come. We will see what the elders have decided."

Pressing her lips together, Milcah tasted blood. She followed Mahlah out of their ramskin dwelling in a procession as serious as when they petitioned Moses for their land.

That day they had received a blessing from God. This night, a storm shadowed her future and her inheritance.

A turbulent storm named Eli ben Abishua.

7

Men's voices quieted as she, Mahlah, and Tirzah sauntered toward a broad-shouldered group of clansmen. Praise be that Mahlah took her time, strolling as if she, not Joshua, led their people. Milcah's belly hollowed. Rarely had she received a reprimand in life. Tongue lashings were bestowed on her older sisters. Some within reason. Now, she had to explain ending up under Eli's form. Would the truth be accepted by her clan?

Elders of Manasseh surrounded Reuben, Keenan, and Eli's father. Noah's husband hovered a few feet from the squabbling. What a shame Jeremiah was mute. His calm, perceptive wisdom went unheard.

Mahlah clapped her hands in a celebratory rhythm.

Heads turned.

"We have waited long enough to see if a betrothal has been offered for my sister." Mahlah came alongside Milcah. "As you can see, my sister was injured when our clansman fell. What have your discussions brought forth?"

Reuben marched forward and joined his wife. Tirzah hid behind Reuben's sizeable form.

No other elder came alongside Milcah for comfort.

Had Eli even made an offer for her? Briefly, she closed her eyes and prayed. *Lord, give me insight and guide my steps.*

She scrunched her toes in her sandals and drew to her full, unassuming height. "Where is Eli ben Abishua? Has he taken responsibility for our...for his fall?"

"I have." The deep confession came from behind the group of elders.

Keenan shifted closer to his father. Eli's frame became visible. Hunched, he sat on a rock, blood oozing from his mouth.

Had he been struck? His mouth had fared better than hers from his flattening of her bones. Did Eli need convincing to offer a betrothal? Why did so much fear surround her reputation?

Abishua strutted toward Mahlah and Reuben.

"My son will offer for your sister." Abishua dipped his head in her direction. "Eli will send livestock to his brother to uphold the contract." Abishua barely acknowledged Jeremiah, his youngest son. "May the union happen before we set out to claim our portions."

"No." Milcah's retort ignited a shocked rumbling among her elders.

Swallowing, she continued her protest. "My youngest sister is to be wed soon. She has waited since last spring. We will arrange her celebration before mine. How can I take care of a husband when I am not yet settled on my land?"

Abishua tapped his fingers together. "Without a husband, you will not have your land for long."

Where did Abishua's loyalty lie? If she did not inherit her land, it would mean his third son had perished. Like the others. Memories of Hanoch threatened her composure. She willed her features to overcome her grief. How could a father desire land over the life of a son?

Clutching her ring, she twisted it round and round.

Mahlah gave her a slight wink. "I expect to host two weddings with my husband." Her eldest sister's confident gaze traveled to each man present.

She could not have loved Mahlah more.

"God has seen fit to bless me and my sisters with our father's land," Mahlah said. "I do not believe He will exclude my sister."

Even with his future being bandied about in the night air, Eli didn't speak. Truly, for once in her life, she desired to hear if his folly this night was a scheme or happenstance?

Milcah flexed her feet and stepped closer to the bearded faces and skeptical glances of her elders.

"I ask to speak to my betrothed. Alone."

"With no kin present?" Abishua smirked at Mahlah. Did he insinuate her sister had raised a harlot?

Gathering sticks had brought on this predicament. Nothing more simmered in the dark.

"My brother-in-law, Jeremiah, can stand with us," Milcah reasoned. "Is he not related to both families? One by blood and the other by marriage?" Not to mention Jeremiah's lack of hearing would be a benefit.

Abishua clicked his tongue. "The daughters of Zelophehad are too bold."

"The daughters of Zelophehad are landowners." Reuben spoke plainly, but every muscle in his forearms pulled taut. "We leave tomorrow for the valley. To claim the land Eleazar described at Gilgal."

She would praise Reuben's fortitude later. Pointing at Jeremiah, she motioned for him to join her and Eli. Noah communicated with her husband easily. Fortunately, Jeremiah understood her hand movements and stationed himself at her side.

She drew closer to Eli's perch on the boulder. "Shall we?"

An elder clasped a hand to his chest. "You need to learn your place, woman."

Eli stood. He turned to the elder. "She knows her place. It is in the fertile northern valley."

"If only you live to see it," the elder huffed.

Eli laughed as the elder made his way toward the pointed tent tops of Manasseh. With the sweep of his hand, her betrothed said, "You wanted to talk? I know an oak tree with a wide trunk."

She should scold his amusement at their predicament, but his bloodied mouth drew her pity.

They did, indeed, end up under the branches of the oak. Jeremiah crossed his arms and leaned against the trunk. His gaze stayed steadfast on his brother. Was he curious about the events of this night, too? How much would he understand from studying their lips?

Eli placed his hands behind his head and stretched as if his muscles were as tender as hers. His good eye beheld her with awe and a hint of mischief.

"It should have been more."

"What are you talking about?" She didn't expect him to be the first to speak. That, and being close to his muscular body, one that she had felt upon her skin, caused her distraction.

"Your bride price. It should have been double what I offered." His shoulders slumped ever so slightly. "Too many of our tribesmen are taking my spoils of war across the river."

This was the Eli she knew. Often drunk. Searching out games of chance. Vanishing when work needed to be done.

"I'm not concerned about the livestock." Harsh was

her confession, but who could blame her after the pain and distress caused by her clansman.

"You aren't?" Eli dug at the dirt with his sandal. His gaze danced between her and the ground. The pit in the dirt won his attention.

"My land concerns me." She crossed her arms and focused on his sandal. He had big feet. Too bad they didn't balance well in a tree. "How will I…how will we work my land? I want to bring praise to my father's name. I want my sisters to be proud of my work. I want God to be proud."

"That's no small feat with me as your betrothed." He attempted a smile and failed.

Would she get any answers from Eli? "Why do you say that?"

His one-eyed gaze met her full on. "Who's proud of me? I drink too much. Most of my wealth is gone. Even a pagan scarred my face."

"You fought with Joshua for our land."

"Not very well."

"Yet you survived." The slick gold of Hanoch's gift itched upon her finger. If only Hanoch had survived the battles. The pound of her heart in her ears silenced the chirps and chatter of the night. Didn't Eli understand that they would face the future as man and wife? She had loved an honorable man and desired to love another.

"I'm not asking for much, Eli. I need you to do one thing well. I need you to work fertile fields and give the first fruits to God." Her breaths stuttered. "Can you do that?"

He stared and did not flinch.

"For me?"

Jeremiah stepped toward her and Eli, hands fisted. Veins ridged in her brother-in-law's neck.

She held up her hand, flat, to her brother-in-law. Pointing at Eli, she pretended to stumble. "No more drunkenness." She made sure her betrothed was listening as she motioned for Jeremiah. "Or casting lots for chance." Picking up a stone, she shook it, and let it roll toward Jeremiah's feet.

Eli glanced at his youngest brother. His head bobbed in agreement.

Jeremiah might be younger, but he could match anyone in strength. Jeremiah stepped backward. And before she knew it, Eli's attention returned. Her betrothed had slouched like a haggard old man before the elders, but for a moment, she saw a flicker of something. Was it hope? Vigor for new possibilities? Relief that he had lived?

Eli moved closer, his back to his brother. "I will try to do what you ask."

Warmth from his broad body seeped closer to her weary limbs. She tamped down any thought of what the end of their betrothal would bring.

"Will you ever tell me why you were up in that tree?"

"Does it matter?" He beheld the starry sky as if he was actually considering an answer. "I didn't think I had much of a future in Canaan. Now, I have a betrothed, land, and—"

"And what?" Her clipped words revealed her vanishing patience.

With a mischievous spark in his eye, he bowed before her. "I have only to make something grow."

8

The next morning, Milcah rolled onto her side. Her muscles protested every move. Of course they did. She had broken Eli's fall from the oak. The nightmare from the previous hours was her reality. How many times did the daughters of Zelophehad need to kindle gossip? Forced betrothals did not uphold the reputation of the woman. Her name would be sullied. The sooner she and her sisters got on the move, the better.

Glancing at the sunlight dotting the seam in the ramskin above her mat, she prayed. "Lord, I have followed You all of my life, but I don't understand why all this heartache is happening to me. Help me to understand Your ways."

Tirzah poked her head inside the tent. "Mahlah is already packed. Hurry. We can gather our pegs."

Milcah groaned. "Our sister did not get pummeled by a rock of a man." She arched her stiff back.

"I know rocks," Tirzah said. "Eli is no rock. He is a fat boar."

"Sister." Milcah tried to reprimand Tirzah's insult. "Do not say such things about an elder clansman. Didn't he fight for our land?"

"Eli isn't here. Not when there is work to be done." Tirzah pulled a face and vanished from the tent flap.

Milcah shook her head. What would she do with herself when Tirzah married? She doubted Eli would flood her dwelling with opinions and demands so early in the day.

She brushed her long, matted hair, donned a head covering, and ducked out of the tent.

"Good. You have risen," Mahlah called. Amos and Abigail ran around the cart while Jonah loaded crates. "Reuben would like to leave soon. The animals will fare better in the cool of the day."

Not to mention her children.

"I will help straightaway." Milcah stretched and marched to assist her sister.

A woman approached. The gold bracelets on her wrists glistened as she opened her arms. Her striped veil draped across her chin, hiding portions of her face.

"You cannot leave without a kiss," the woman said with a bit of a muffle. She headed toward Mahlah and revealed her features with a tug on her veil. "Does my brother not care about his sister? Am I not an orphan now?" Reuben's sister Basemath pouted.

Where was her sympathy when we were orphaned? Milcah's compassion was running low. Her own woes were forefront in her mind.

Forgive me, God.

"Good morning, Basemath. We surely know how you feel." Milcah nodded toward her eldest sister. Weren't Basemath's fingernails bloodying Mahlah's arm shortly after their own father had perished?

Basemath swiped at her cheek with dramatic emphasis. Her jewelry clanked as her wrist rotated.

Tirzah halted her attack on the tent pegs. She grabbed an empty waterskin and jogged passed their visitor.

When had the youngest daughter of Zelophehad been so eager to do work?

"Shalom." Tirzah puckered briefly, imitating a kiss. "I have many unfinished chores."

Basemath clung to Mahlah. "I will be all alone when my brother settles north."

Milcah hesitantly aided in the comfort of Mahlah's sister-in-law. She didn't need onlookers believing the grief was over Milcah's recent betrothal.

Most of her life, she and her sisters had slept a tent away from Reuben and his family. All her sisters had wept at Susanna's passing. Reuben's mother had possessed a tender heart. Her husband died less than a year after his wife. Three years had passed since Nemuel's death, but traveling into Canaan without her neighbors or the safety of their familiar camp left Milcah tamping down the fears of an unknown land. Perhaps Basemath shared those fears.

"Where is your husband's family going?" Milcah rubbed Basemath's back.

"We do not have to travel far." Basemath sniffled. "We are settling by the Jordan River."

"Near Shiloh then? Reuben will see you when he comes to the Tabernacle." Milcah smiled at her forlorn neighbor. "Do not worry. We will see you at Tirzah's wedding and then my own."

"Your wedding?" Basemath cocked her head and beheld Mahlah with a furrowed brow. "Why haven't I heard of this arrangement? Am I forgotten so easily?"

"It only happened last night." Mahlah's smile fell flat.

Basemath's lashes blinked. Was she scrolling through a list of eligible clansmen in her mind?

"Is he old?" Basemath asked.

"Why would you assume such a thing." Milcah stepped away from their visitor and wrapped an arm around her aching side.

"When you have lived a long life, you don't fear death as much." Basemath patted Milcah's shoulder. "Your other suitors have not fared well."

Mahlah shifted beside her, forming a wall of sisterhood.

Teeth clenched, Milcah gathered her sweetest morning voice. "I am to wed Eli ben Abishua."

"But you were the sensible sister. Meek and quiet." Basemath let her utterance hang in the air as she whirled to face Mahlah. "Why would you or my brother allow such an arrangement?" Her tone harshened.

Amos and Abigail stopped playing and stared at their aunt. "A man like Eli will cause trouble. Verily, this pairing will be muttered about all over Shiloh. Must I endure more gossip about my brother's wife and her sisters?"

Milcah's cheeks flamed. Why should she worry about Canaanite neighbors in the valley? Could they be any worse than Basemath and her callous tongue?

"Sister." Reuben's booming voice was a welcome interruption. "Have you seen Noah and Hoglah this morn?" He eyed his wife and gave a slight shrug.

"I can't traipse through dung in my condition." Basemath smoothed a hand over her rounding stomach. "As I hear, I will see you at a wedding. Possibly two."

"Definitely two." Milcah's muscles burned and not from her collision with Eli.

"I will pray as so." Basemath sighed and fanned her face with her hand. "I must be on my way. My husband does not like me to wander far since I could be carrying his heir."

As Basemath passed her brother, she cupped a hand to her lips. Her crafted whisper carried. "She was the well-behaved one. Why is she bound to that troublemaker? I say, what sins did Abishua and his wife commit to birth a mute and a fool."

Mahlah's mouth gaped.

Milcah stood slack-jawed as well. Forget the aches, her muscles burned hotter than a torch.

"Until the wedding, then." Milcah gave a brief head bob and turned her back on Basemath. She fought a single tear from falling. She would do what her sisters had done all of their lives and go forth with God. And if God saw fit, she'd go forth with Eli as a husband.

No matter what she faced in the northern valley, chariots, war, or toil, she couldn't leave Shiloh fast enough. Truly, it was time to move on and lay eyes on the fields that awaited tilling.

As she traipsed toward her tent, raven-haired Amos sprinted toward her. Her nephew jumped to a stop at her side. He had inherited Mahlah's boldness.

"Who's a fool?" His bright brown eyes held an innocence as to the meaning of his aunt's words.

Milcah laughed at his curiosity. "I don't know. I don't know any fools."

She prayed she spoke the truth.

9

Six days had passed since her future had become bound to a notorious clansman. For six days, she had traveled the ridge route north. For six days, she marched in the dust of the herds. Herds of animals and the herd of her tribesmen. The anxiousness of her betrothal faded like last week's dream. She hadn't spoken to Eli in six days. Would he work and cherish her land as she would? Or would she bemoan the day she wed a troublemaker? Basemath was probably bemoaning it herself to all who would listen in Shiloh.

Milcah couldn't blame Eli solely for his absence. Reuben had thought it best for Eli to assist Jeremiah with the livestock. Jeremiah and his son, Daniel, had welcomed the oversight of another shepherd. With Eli occupied, she watched over Mahlah's children while her eldest sister drove the cart filled with wares and the occasional sleeping helper. Tirzah led the camels, stopping only to claim an appropriately sized rock for her sling. Hoglah rarely made an appearance. She stayed with her husband's herds. Milcah wished her sister would rid herself of the past. Offerings had covered her and Eli's sin in the worship pit of a false god.

When evening fell, Milcah stacked plates and cups in the cart. The mundane chore was a celebration, for tomorrow she would glimpse her piece of the valley.

Pebbles crunched near the wooden breeches of the cart.

She glanced in the direction of the sound, and gasped. "Eli?"

He grasped the side of the cart leaving wooden slats as a barrier between their bodies.

"You are working late." His eye held the spark of an amber-orange dawn, and he bestowed that spark on her.

"Eli, we are alone." She scanned the surroundings to see if her sisters were aware of his arrival. She and her betrothed were unattended.

"Mahlah is not far." He dipped his head in the direction of the tents. His mane of hair had been banded. "The wood separates us. It's not as if I could topple over this." He grinned and gave the slat a shake. He and Jeremiah had the same rugged jaw, but with Eli there was always the hint of whimsy.

"We have been separated for six days." The truth came out as a rebuke. Maybe too much so. She didn't want him to think that she was bothered by his absence. She had her sisters for companionship.

"Aw." Eli's hand slid over the top of the wooden slat. "I am not accustomed to working from first light to sundown. My brother and your sister have large herds to move."

"Noah has been growing Father's herds since she was a child." She straightened the stack of cups and remembered how God had blessed the efforts of an orphan.

"I remember. We avoided her so as not to receive a

lash from her whip."

"Noah would not have harmed you?"

"Are you sure?" He leaned forward and winked. The perpetual gleam in his eye made her belly float. Where was a curious niece or nephew when she needed one? "I did not carry out my duties as a son should. Avoiding a bunch of sheep was easier than herding them."

She bit her lip. A small sting reminded her of her injury from his fall.

"What if I inherit grazing land?"

He tapped a rhythm on the wood. "Then I will need my stubborn ox and butting goats back from Jeremiah."

Was settling the Promised Land of God a game to him? Her throat thickened. Hanoch toiled over his father's flocks and gave his life in battle for Canaan. Why had God allowed a lazy kinsman to be her husband and not Hanoch? Pressure pulsed behind her eyes. She blinked and willed her sorrow to stay tamped down.

"It is late." She dipped her head so he would not see her angst. "The children will rise early." She drew backward to take her leave.

"Don't go." Eli rushed around the side of the cart. "I was speaking of the past. Tomorrow we will head into the valley and begin our future." He held out his hands as if he was measuring her width. "I have been thinking on the trail."

Eli contemplative? "About what?"

"How God blessed the daughters of a man who lacked judgment—"

Her mouth gaped as a surge of indignation roared through her body. How could he utter such an insult? "One time, Eli. My father grumbled against God one time. He paid for it with his life." She rocked on her sandals.

"Then there is hope for me." He reached for her and

halted his hand.

Slapping him entered her mind, but then another touch could have his family demanding a quick union. How was she going to settle her land with Eli? One moment he was endearing and the next infuriating. A shiver blanketed her arms.

Tirzah plopped her head on Milcah's shoulder.

"I wondered what was taking so long. Praise be I found you both upright. I don't think Mahlah would believe you fell again, Eli." Tirzah's giggle was not at all comforting.

"Eli was leaving." Devoid of any emotion, she held his stare. "He shouldn't have come here." Oh, why couldn't Eli have stayed away for another day?

Eli dipped his head. "You will see. I am ready to accept a blessing from God."

He didn't retreat. He stayed, beholding her as if they had planned to be together for many years.

With insides wound tighter than a knot, she turned, grabbed hold of Tirzah's hand, and stomped toward her tent.

"What were you discussing?" Tirzah's breaths quickened as she tried to keep pace with her sister.

"Someone's lack of judgment." In her most serious voice, she added, "And it wasn't my own."

~*~

The next morning Milcah rose early to help bake the morning bread. The scent of ash and flame told her that Mahlah had beaten her to the task.

As Milcah neared the small fire pit, Mahlah held out a

flower.

"Eli brought this by a bit ago. He had to leave to help Jeremiah water the herds." Mahlah's smile was way too bright for this hour of dawn. "He said to tell you it was a lily of the valley."

Milcah plucked the blossom from her sister's hands and breathed in the sweet, innocent scent of the lily.

Holding the flower over the fire, she dropped it into the flame.

If only the bud had been a sign from God about her land, and not a peace offering from Eli. Maybe then she would have accepted it.

10

While on a short rest from their journey, Milcah breathed in the cool breeze that consumed the valley. Had the wind traveled from the Great Sea? Reuben should have spoken of the magnificence of their new home. Green patchwork hues covered the hillsides and mountains. Did Reuben believe boasting about his wife's inheritance would be shameful? Or was he worried about another tribesman challenging Mahlah's right of ownership?

On either side of the westward path, pine, oak, palm, and eucalyptus trees joined in a marvel of forest. Would Eli need to clear trees from her portion of land? What if she owned an olive grove? Her spirit soared over the highest slope of Mount Gilboa. Before the end of this day, she would see God's provision.

"Praise be to the One True God."

Three-year-old Abigail stirred from her drape over Milcah's shoulder.

Mahlah approached. She wore the mustard-hued head covering that had belonged to their mother. The color had faded over the years, though no one would notice with her sister's dark, angled features glowing from beneath the linen.

"I will take my daughter." Mahlah reached for Abigail. "There is room for her to sleep in the cart."

Milcah obliged and dislodged the warm body from her shoulder.

"I do not know how your daughter sleeps with the bustle of herds and kinsmen about."

"She has brothers." Mahlah grinned, and then her lips pressed thin. "Do you still agree to Tirzah and Hoglah's arrangement with the land? You do not have to settle the farthest portion."

"Our arrangement is best." Hadn't she always been the keeper of peace? "I do not need Enid and Lamech stampeding their livestock over my land."

Mahlah grinned. She leaned in for a kiss. "Your betrothed has finally returned." She backstepped with her daughter. "I must consult with Reuben on how far we have to travel."

Eli strolled forward with a hand hidden behind his tunic and acknowledged Mahlah with a bob of his head. His brown hair had been lightened by dust dislodged by hooves, carts, and sandals.

"Shalom." He bowed and extended a bulky, linen-wrapped gift.

"You already left me a present." Which she had burned.

"We are not in Gilgal anymore. I am sure you saw the chariot on the hill as we entered the valley." His hand trembled as the gift stayed suspended between them.

"You're shaking." Was he a nervous bridegroom?

"Ah." Eli grinned like a boy in need of a scold. "My sister-in-law serves me water and goat's milk. Not wine."

So much for Eli being shy about his shortcomings. She would have to praise Noah for her oversight.

"Milk and water are fine drinks. Especially if the livestock you are moving have sharp horns." Milcah tipped her head and withheld a welcoming smile.

"Are you going to open it?" He indicated the cloth. "There are whispers that I may not see my wedding night. My gift will make sure that you live to have a husband."

"So, it's not another lily?" She smiled and began unwrapping the linen.

Coiled beneath the cloth was a leather belt with a sheathed knife attached. Never in her nineteen years would she have guessed to receive such a token from a beloved. Did he expect her to slay Canaanites?

"Eli, I will not be able to oversee a household with this knife on my hip." She flipped the dagger for him to receive it, hilt first.

"Keep it near." He made no motion to accept the knife. "A few men still live in these cities. They may seek revenge for the lives of their dead kings."

She tucked the weapon under her arm. "The descendants of Joseph are numerous. We have moved more dirt from these roads than a sandstorm. Only fools would challenge our tribesmen and our God."

"True." He edged forward, closing what respectable distance Mahlah would allow. "Now we have women and children to protect. I will protect you, Milcah bat Zelophehad."

Her thoughts scattered. Had Eli ever spoken her name before? In such a tender tone? He had swept into her life like a flighty bird, and now he was acting like a swan. What had Noah done to this man?

When she realized he was beholding her, she cleared her throat.

"I promise to keep the knife close, Eli." His name faltered in her throat. "Though, I do not believe God would give us this land and permit idol-worshipers to reclaim it. My sisters and I have always walked with God."

"As have I." Eli did not sound as sure. "I am ready to fight for your land if need be."

"Let us hope there is no need."

A noise like a continuous cough sounded behind her.

Eli peered over her shoulder. "Your older sisters have arrived from taking care of the flocks."

Without turning, she knew beyond reason who was making her displeasure known. Hoglah.

"I shall go help Jeremiah," Eli said, his eye downcast.

"Don't go," she whispered. "We are heading off to see our land soon. Don't you want to know how much work comes along with my inheritance?" She brought forth his gift. "We could always use this as a trowel."

11

Milcah clapped a hand over her mouth. Had she ever been so excited that her stomach heaved with nothing to show for its dissatisfaction? She was tempted to slide from her donkey and race forward to glimpse her land. First things first. Mahlah was the oldest daughter, and she and Reuben would claim the inheritance of their fathers on the easternmost edge of the valley.

Eli rode beside Milcah, straight-backed and serious, except for when she would catch him gazing at her profile. Then, he would stifle a smirk and return to his solemn stature. She did not want to draw the ire of Hoglah or seem provocative to her intended by inviting conversation with him. Today was about her land. The birthright of her father. The blessing bestowed by the One True God on orphaned sisters. No matter if the land needed much work, or little, she would praise God for His provision.

"Your nerves may need some honey," Eli said, his voice calm, but holding a hint of curiosity.

"I will be dancing with delight at the end of our ride, so no balm is needed at the moment." She wished Reuben would hurry and hammer a stake to mark the beginning of their plots.

Urging his mount closer, Eli said, "I see you are wearing your trowel."

"I am ready to go to work." His gift weighed heavy upon her hip. She should have packed it, but she did not know if Canaanites would have laid claim to her land. As they moved westward, the beleaguered city of Megiddo rose higher over the plains. Her provision would be closest to the idol-worshiping city.

"Once I settle my inheritance, I shall not be moved from my land." She dipped her chin. No matter what may come, Eli's death, or Keenan's schemes, or a battle with pagans, her feet would remain firmly planted in this valley.

"In all my years, I have never known you to speak on a whim." Eli re-established the distance between their donkeys.

She leaned closer to him. "You do not know me that well, Eli."

"I will. And I am looking forward to the remedy." His features held almost no expression. Not imp, nor angel. She should scold his tongue, but woe if he hadn't rendered her speechless. She willed her flesh not to shade scarlet.

Reuben and another elder of Manasseh rode forward to the edge of the path to the sea. Truly, her brother-in-law chose an appropriate time to begin the proceedings. Eli would have to be quiet.

Her sisters and their husbands looked on from their mounts as Reuben dismounted.

"I shall claim the farthest forest as the heir of Nemuel," Reuben said. "We can clear the land if our herds grow too large. Mahlah's land will begin at the far creek and go until that nub of a hill." Reuben searched his sisters-in-law's faces, and beheld his wife's. No dissent came.

Tears flowed down Mahlah's cheeks. "Praise the God of Abraham, Isaac, and Jacob. This portion is fitting for my family."

"Then let us hurry onward." Noah kicked her mount. "Jeremiah and I are ready to build pens and assess the grazing land for our livestock."

Their blessed party passed the nub of a hill and halted their mounts a distance from the landmark.

Noah surveyed the land before her. She slipped from her donkey, making sure her babe did not waken in the linen sling that crossed her chest. She strolled a ways onto her inheritance and squinted into the distance.

"There are two pools and an oak. The branches are strong enough to hold my slings and my injured animals." Noah's joyous laughter carried. Travelers on the way of the sea slowed their journeys. Some Manassites called out in Hebrew to celebrate with Noah and Jeremiah.

Jeremiah joined his wife. Sinking to his knees, he raised his arms toward the cloudless sky.

Noah pointed to a leaning eucalyptus tree. "May that tree and its seedling be our dividing line." Noah turned her attention to Hoglah. "Do you agree?"

Hoglah nodded in agreement. "You are giving me the grove of olive trees?"

"Truly, Sister." Noah sauntered toward Hoglah. "You will need to produce the oil for cooking. Bring some extra bread my way while you are at it."

"You are too generous." Lamech leaned from his donkey. "Our fields are as lush as yours. We have no complaints with this allotment. We are blessed beyond measure."

Hoglah buried her face in her head covering. Sobs leaked from the folds of the cloth. Her sister's whole body shook. Was it glee over her fields? Or the worries of a barren womb?

Milcah dismounted and rested her cheek in Hoglah's lap. "God is shining His face upon us. I trust He will give you sons and daughters to work this land and to help birth many, many new lambs."

"I pray for that blessing as well." Lamech smiled as tears streaked to his beard.

Hoglah nearly crushed Milcah's hand. "I've been praying for a babe for years. Where is my answer?"

"It will come." Milcah met her sister's tear-filled dark eyes. "I have questioned God on many things, but I do not lose sight that He is God. My heart has been heavy, and now it is uncertain. May it ever beat in obedience to our God."

Hoglah nodded. "I shouldn't burden you. Not on this day of blessing."

"You can burden me anytime." Milcah kissed her sister's hand. "The yolk of my sisters is light."

"Not so much the yolk of your betrothed." Prune-mouthed, Hoglah indicated Eli with a tip of her head.

How would Milcah ever build trust between Eli and Hoglah?

"Hurry," Tirzah called. "Where does my land end?"

Tirzah and Enid raced their donkeys toward her inheritance.

When would her youngest sister learn patience? Couldn't Tirzah see Hoglah's pain?

Milcah stroked the mane of Hoglah's donkey. "Do not grow weary of petitioning God for a child. How many years did Rachel inquire of God before she conceived our forefather Joseph?" She brushed a tear from her own cheek. "Now, I fear we must keep up with Tirzah. Our sister is much too quick for us."

"Perhaps for you, old woman." Hoglah urged her donkey into a trot.

Milcah laughed. "I am younger than you."

Eli, atop his mount, came alongside her. He held the lead to her beast. Her future husband's features appeared jovial as if he understood the banter she had enjoyed with Hoglah. Had she ever seen Eli lighthearted? Not without a jug of wine.

Up ahead, Tirzah motioned for everyone to hurry.

"We have shade for the animals," Tirzah yelled, her voice squeaking from giddiness. "Come and see. My land is a maze of trees."

"You will help us clear some of them, won't you, Lamech?" Enid's enthusiasm had his brother shaking his head.

Lamech leapt from his mount, ran, and embraced his brother. "We have cousins not as fortunate as we. They can fell some of your shade. God has fit our lands together better than I believed possible."

"Toda raba, Milcah. You will be blessed for your generosity." Tirzah swung herself around the trunk of a young oak.

Milcah glanced at Eli. He shaded his eyes and stared into the distance. With the tree cover on Tirzah's land, it was almost impossible to see what waited ahead on their portion. Was Eli curious about her inheritance, or was he ignoring the embraces and camaraderie Lamech and his brother shared?

A respected elder of Manasseh maneuvered his ride over by Eli.

"You agree to the younger sister getting her inheritance before the older?" The elder stayed stern-faced. Tirzah's glee had not secured his favor. "Once the land is settled, I will not come back to judge any grievances."

Milcah drew a deep breath and held it. How could the elder ignore her presence? Eli had been her betrothed for days, not months. The silence among her sisters rivaled the dead of night.

Eli cleared his throat.

She hoped he remembered she had a blade on her hip.

"The daughters of Zelophehad should be the ones to decide who claims the land and in what order. I will work my intended's land no matter where it may lie. We have come to an understanding in this matter." Eli cast a glance toward Hoglah and Lamech. He also assessed Mahlah's reaction before beholding his future wife's gaze with his scarred face.

Was that her Eli talking? He spoke as an elder or priest, not the maligned drunkard among Abishua's sons.

"I do not believe I could have spoken our wishes better." She bowed briefly before the elder. "I do not desire to be a thorn between brothers or to cause distress among my sisters. God has seen fit to keep me without a husband until recently." She indicated Eli, perched on his mount. "I will be pleased with whatever portion I receive."

"Very well. Let us carry on." The elder sidestepped closer. "I have overseen the battles for Megiddo, Taanach, and Beth-Shan. I have toiled many a day in this valley. I am sure you will see that voicing this agreement one more time is in your interest." The elder's expression sobered. "Dissension comes swiftly into families where arrangements are not stated among witnesses."

She bobbed her head in agreement.

Her tribal leader pressed his lips together as if suppressing more wisdom. His gaze flitted between Milcah and Eli. "I trust you will be hospitable to your kinsmen."

"Always." Perhaps it was her time to run toward her

inheritance? The elder's demeanor had her heartbeat rising like a frothy wave on the sea. Why hadn't he asked her sisters about hospitality?

Eli held out his hand. "May your donkey and mine charge to our home."

"Home." The rumble of that word on her lips made her spirit soar.

She turned to address her sisters. "I cannot see ahead past the trees. Forgive my impatience while we leave you in our dust."

"Not so fast," Reuben said in his sovereign voice. "We have yet to set a boundary between your land and Tirzah's." Reuben and Mahlah scanned the terrain with furrowed brows.

"I believe there is a substantial hill." Mahlah indicated a grassy dome with no tree cover. "God has created a sizeable boundary between my sisters' portions. Shall we see what lies ahead?"

Milcah kicked her mount and trotted forward. *Bounce, bounce, bounce.* She almost regretted her hurried approach. As the path inclined, her donkey's enthusiasm waned, and he slowed to a fast walk.

Farther and farther up the way to the sea, she traveled. The conquered city of Megiddo loomed over the lush valley. The stark alabaster and brown stones of the fortress contrasted with the emerald hues of the fertile plain below.

Even now, her mouth parched at the image of Reuben, Lamech, and Eli advancing to lay siege to such a stronghold. Her bones grew heavy at the sight of the stone wall. Megiddo's wall had not crumbled like Jericho's. Only by the power of the One True God could Joshua and Israel have claimed victory. Every morning, she would be reminded of the greatness of her God.

Eli charged forth. Onward he rode, past the landmark

hill separating her allotment from Tirzah's. Instead of bellowing a description of the land, he became a stone rider as his mount slowed. Was uttering a single word too difficult?

What could silence her betrothed? Rocky fields needing a plow? Forests of wide-trunked trees needing to be cleared? Barren land? She almost *tsked* out loud at his silence.

She passed the last grove of Tirzah's trees and glimpsed what lay beyond the grassy dividing mound. Her mouth gaped. The breeze chilling her lips could have blown her all the way to the Great Sea.

Before her, arranged in row upon perfect row, lay a vineyard. A vast vineyard. A vineyard the likes of which she had not seen in all of Canaan. Certainly, she had not beheld such a sight wandering in the wilderness.

Dismounting, she strolled trance-like through a clearing, down a grassy slope, and toward trellised vines. Vines tall, stout, and rooted like small trees. Tirzah's squealing didn't even cause her concern. She watched her footing lest she trample her abundance. An abundance of plants ripe with grape clusters that cascaded over rolling hills.

Crouching, she plucked a grape. Its skin rolled easily upon her fingers as if it knew her, belonged to her. Tossing the grape into her mouth, she bit down. The succulent sour taste of her fruit impressed her tongue, but the grape flesh lodged in her throat. God had granted her a vineyard. A vineyard that would make wine a plenty. Wine her husband consumed to excess. How was she going to honor God with a vineyard? Didn't God care that her portion could cause her marital woe?

Eli bent near a cluster of low hanging grapes. Her betrothed wouldn't need to grow anything. Their vineyard was vibrant and green and ready for harvest.

Tirzah shrieked and danced, hopping side to side at the edge of a small clearing. Her sister raised something overhead and raced closer, her prized possession held firmly aloft.

"Sister, you are so blessed." Tirzah's giggle echoed over the fields. "You have a patch of melons!"

12

Melons were the least of Milcah's worries. Learning how to produce wine and learning how to keep her betrothed from consuming their abundance and passing out drunk, were foremost in her mind.

She bit her lip. How could she not be thankful for her bountiful inheritance? The grapes were ripe and round. A stone press waited to be filled. Plants draped the valley in hues of green and purple. Everything waited for a winemaker. Except, she did not know how to produce wine.

Tirzah cradled the round melon as if it were a gold nugget. "We must serve some at my wedding."

Her sister must have meant the melon for it would take time for the grapes to ferment into wine.

Milcah unsheathed her knife. "Why don't you offer some melon to the men? They are studying the winepress. The stone wall will give you leverage for a clean cut."

Tirzah grinned and accepted the blade. "Since when do you carry a weapon? Did Hoglah give you that to keep Eli away?"

"Don't tell stories about me." Hoglah sauntered closer

with Mahlah and Noah. "Though if I had thought you needed protection from Eli, I would have given you Lamech's sword." Hoglah indicated the men congregated by the winepress. "Serve them some fruit and save a piece for me."

"This is the sister I know. Ordering me to work." Tirzah sashayed toward the circular stone pit with her fat melon.

Mahlah cocooned Milcah in an embrace.

"Why aren't you dancing with Tirzah? Your inheritance is a sight to behold."

Why wasn't she feeling joyous? She should be praising God, but a family with many sons would struggle to manage such a property. She was an unmarried woman with a disputed reputation.

Milcah rested her head on Mahlah's shoulder. "I am delighted with my inheritance. Truly." Her assurance didn't convince her own heart. "All our lands are a sight to behold, but father never prepared us for winemaking." She scanned the magnitude of her blessing. "Where will I get workers to pick the grapes? How will I store the wine? I will need to buy jars." Her eyes welled with tears.

"Hey." Noah's beauty filled Milcah's vision. "Have we ever left you alone? We will assist you in any way we can."

"You have families and—"

"And where do you think we will get our laborers?" Noah rotated her leather bracelet. "I can pick grapes." She caressed Miriam's ringlets. "Miriam may try to pick a few herself."

Hoglah wedged into their sister-huddle. "Why don't we dry some of the grapes? I can make raisin cakes. We will sell them to every traveler on the route west."

Milcah blinked with surprise. "You don't like Eli. You

do not like being near him?"

Hoglah flapped her hand dismissively. "That was before you inherited a vineyard. I don't mind watching Eli toil. Hard work will do him good. I will make him load and unload my grapes."

"Our sister is offering to make cakes for us. Accept it," Noah said. "Her husband and Enid wanted adjoining lands. You can blame her for your abundance." Noah winked at their middle sister. "Didn't Lamech mention he has cousins?"

"Many who will work for wages." Hoglah strolled over by the melon patch. "I can set up a cooking fire here and keep track of how long our kin work." She raised a conspiratorial eyebrow. "When Eli comes for his bread, I will make sure his hands are calloused. His feet better be dyed a deep shade of purple."

Milcah tilted her face toward the late afternoon sun. "Toda raba, Adonai. What would I do without my sisters?"

Mahlah grasped Milcah's and Noah's hands. "We will do whatever we can to help, but we have families to take care of. You will need to talk to Eli and make sure he is able to manage the workload. He does not come from a line of winemakers either."

Noah's captivating features sobered. "I believe Jeremiah would be happy to see his brother have a purpose. Eli has been lost now that the battles are through."

"I will talk to him." Milcah lifted baby Miriam into the air and relished her squeals of delight. "Perhaps Eli knows more about winemaking than we know?

She could only hope.

13

Mahlah and Reuben agreed to leave Milcah and Eli in the vineyard for a discussion. Reuben made it clear that without a chaperone, he expected everyone to uphold the honor of their families. If Milcah did not return by the moon's brilliance, her brothers-in-law would come with swords and elders. Eli assured everyone that their sole act would be conversing about her inheritance.

Was Eli content with the labor ahead? She would soon find out.

She joined Eli by the elevated stone basin in which, if they could hire laborers, their grapes would be trampled. Climbing the stone steps, she beheld the treading floor. Two men the size of Eli could lie toe to head on the mosaic of stone. She suspected the opening in the center of the stone was for the juice to flow through to the pool below.

"It would have been nice if they had left us jars, or even a few skins." She shaded her eyes from the fading sunlight and cast a glance at Eli.

His neck craned toward a wooden structure set above the treading floor.

Was he ignoring her?

Her betrothed chuckled.

Nothing she had said would warrant a laugh. Her back arched at the insult.

He scrubbed his chin. "They tie ropes to the wood to keep the workers from falling into the juice." His good eye cast all its deep brown mystery upon her. "I know where we can get a coil of rope."

"I don't think that is humorous." She did not match his grin. She stared at row upon row of grapes. "I am overwhelmed by my inheritance. Look at the fields and the bounty God has bestowed on us. How can we begin to manage this land when the harvest is upon us?" She shook her head. A few strands of hair dislodged from her covering.

Eli scrutinized the hillside above her head without answering her concerns.

"Say something. You are a man of few words, and you still haven't told me why you were in a tree." She pressed her lips thin as she strolled along the grassy hill dividing her property from Tirzah's. Twisting the gold band she had received from Hanoch, she wondered if her worries would be as numerous if he was standing beside her. She had trusted Hanoch to do his best for her. He was predictable, and work did not scare him. Eli's intentions were a mystery.

Eli sauntered beside her, leaving a respectable distance.

"I was trying to find a purpose."

His words did not make sense. "In a tree?"

"This is hard enough without interruptions." His gaze strayed to the vast mound.

"I am ready to listen."

He raised a bushy eyebrow.

"Well, mostly." Truly, the man had not grown up with

sisters.

Turning toward the fields, Eli crossed his arms and stared. "Your sisters celebrated your inheritance. They did not argue about the wealth in this vineyard or disregard the arrangement of lands. Your sister danced in your melon patch."

Visions of Tirzah's wild dance caused Milcah to smile. "Tirzah has always loved melons. And she is excited about her wedding."

"That is foreign to me." Eli stood as unmovable as the stone winepress.

Her skin tingled. "You are unhappy about our betrothal?" Why did her heart have to clench with ache?

"Oh, no." He joined her by the hill and stepped close, a little too close. He back-stepped and clasped his hands as if remembering Reuben's warning. "I grow happier by the day with our betrothal. I hope you believe me."

How could she not believe him? She had never seen him so exuberant. In the twilight, his rugged features, untamed hair, and vulnerable tone made her desire a niece or nephew's presence. Where were the childish interruptions when one needed them? Warring these past few years had made Eli quite manly.

"Are you listening?" His mouth quirked to one side.

"Yes." She licked her lips, and woe if he did not gaze upon her mouth. She sauntered a few steps forward with the hill on one side and Eli on the other.

"My eldest brother rarely leaves his wife." Eli's truth stunned her. She seldom heard anyone speak of Abishua's heir.

"My brother abides with his wife and my mother, mostly. My father believes it is a sign of weakness. The praise that should have been heaped upon his firstborn, my father bestows on Keenan. He lauds his forcefulness—

"

"And his schemes?" Her disgust with Keenan would not stay hidden.

"My father turns a blind eye. I do not believe he is a conspirator." Eli halted and motioned for them to turn back toward the press. "Keenan gives my father a reason to boast. When Jeremiah was born mute, the gossip gave my father all the more reason to praise Keenan's prowess."

Her bones grew weary listening to Abishua's faults. What if her own father had praised Mahlah and none other? She loved Mahlah, but would she have been content to be dismissed and forgotten by her father?

"Your father never praised you?" The admission was more statement than question.

Eli perched a sandal on the winepress wall. "He never knew me. To get my father's attention, I caused trouble. Better some attention from an elder of Manasseh than none at all."

She glanced at the wood above the treading floor. "So, you were in the tree…?"

"Pondering what Canaan held for me. Was I to work my father's land for his heir or Keenan? Jeremiah had your sister's land. A beautiful family. What future did this land promise me?"

"And now you have something." Nervously, she fingered Hanoch's ring. Was she Eli's revenge on his family? A means to a better end? Turning, she continued traipsing along the grassy hill.

"You own this land. It is your father's." Eli pronounced her inheritance boldly. In a few strides, he caught her. "If we are able to have children, then they will inherit this land." His gaze beheld the mound above her.

His truthful profession eased her fears. A small, but cherished, amount.

"What do you have Eli?"

"You." His chiseled features dimpled. "And the chance to run a profitable vineyard."

Her belly jumped and ran to the far side of her fields. His gaze fell to the dividing mound. Perhaps it was best he did not stare at her in the starlight.

"I don't know how to produce wine. Neither do you." Would he take on the immense responsibility before him?

He stalked toward the winepress and brought a lamp to where she stood. Did he fear Reuben would appear and chastise him?

Eli lifted the lamp above her. "I am no expert, but I am willing to try to learn the process."

Why couldn't he look at her when he was talking about their vineyard? Was grass more interesting than his intended?

She tapped her sandal. "We must get these grapes off the vine, pressed, and into vessels. Soon."

Eli placed his hand upon the hill. His arm was very close to her cheek. Was he finally going to say something to warm her heart like the lamp was warming her skin? She shouldn't have burned his lily. He was agreeing to work, and work hard, in the vineyard.

She tilted her chin toward Eli's face. He was rather tall even without hovering above her in an oak.

"There is a strip of grass on the hill unlike the others." Eli inspected the grass above her head covering while she inspected his distracted gaze. He poked a finger into the blades of grass. "Perhaps there is some clay in the soil."

So much for a kind word from her betrothed. Why couldn't Hanoch be here with her?

Eli flailed his arm. "Something is crawling on my skin." He jiggled faster than Tirzah during her melon dance.

A dark shadow fell to the dirt.

Eli shuffled his feet. "That spider is as big as your sister's melon."

She jerked farther from the hillside. She would not even think about what might be slithering on the ground.

"I doubt your spider was so grand." She swatted at a web tickling the tip of her nose.

In the flickering lamplight, Eli stilled. He placed a finger to his lips.

Was something else living in this hill?

Then, she heard it. The clop of hooves, though faint. Visitors traveled into the clearing and began an ascent toward the press.

Eli blew out their lamp.

In the shadows, she hovered close to Eli. Nothing about this situation was honorable.

She prayed the stranger was one of her sisters' understanding husbands, or that blindness had overtaken the rider.

Eli grasped her arm and pulled her close. "Crouch behind the stones of the press. Do not show yourself no matter what happens to me."

What did he think she was going to do? Announce herself to elders, thieves, or renegade fighters from Megiddo? She had to stay hidden. And stay safe.

"You do have my gift with you?" His whisper rasped with caution.

She nodded.

"Good. Do not be afraid to use it." He tugged her closer to the wall behind the treading floor and left her with the unlit lamp. Moonlight gleamed upon his blade. "I will greet our first guests." The fierceness in his features made her pulse quicken. She had always remembered Eli as the thin-faced fool from her childhood. When had he become such a bold warrior?

Only moments before, her intended had ignored her words and set his interest upon a strip of grass. Now he marched to defend her land and her life. Her skin still remembered his hold upon her arm. Her ears still remembered his warning. And her fluttering belly remembered his possessive stare.

The night remained eerily silent as if she and Eli and their visitors were the only people in all of Canaan. With her back pressed against uneven stones, she did something she hadn't done, ever.

She prayed for Eli ben Abishua by name.

14

"God of Jacob, may my inheritance flow with wine, not blood." She prayed fervently, tucked behind her winepress. Now, that she had claimed her vineyard, no one was going to keep her from making wine. Or marrying. Whichever came first.

"What brings you out on the road after dark?" Eli spoke Hebrew. He knew these visitors, for his question held a welcoming undertone.

"So, it is true? What our elder said. You inherited a vineyard." The sound of muffled claps carried into the night.

She knew that voice. Eli's father had arrived to inspect his son's wealth. His father had finally taken notice of him now he had a vineyard to tend. Though, this vineyard belonged to her father. The daughters of Zelophehad were allotted this portion of the valley. It did not belong to a son of Abishua. Not yet. She should correct their statement of ownership, but then her presence would be known, and her reputation would be cast in doubt, forcing a union. Jaw clenched, she stayed low.

"So, you were not so much the fool for falling on one

of those boastful daughters. I should have attempted such a fall." Keenan's cackle drew her ire. He had tried to drag Noah into his tent by feigning Jeremiah's death. Her sisters followed God and upheld His law among their clan. If only they could have left one dreaded clansman in Shiloh with Basemath.

"You should have chosen the curvy one, brother. You wouldn't have hit the ground so hard." More laughter from Keenan.

"You have already chosen a wife." Eli didn't sound amused. "It is my turn to marry and to begin a family."

"Do not wait long, my son." Abishua's glee disappeared from his greeting. "Our clansmen are already fighting over these fields if you die."

Where was a father's lament over the death of a son?

Footsteps approached the press.

Did Abishua suspect she was here?

God keep them away from the wall. I am not ready to know a man.

She rotated Hanoch's ring on her finger. She would have rushed a celebration if her beloved had lived, but he had been taken from her. Her throat grew thick. No, not now. Stop. Stop. Stop. She needed her wits, not wallowing.

"Most likely the winemaker is dead." Keenan announced the death with a hint of praise. "We did not spare a single warrior's life when we battled for these cities."

"I am the winemaker now. Lift your lamp and follow me. I will show you the pool where we will collect the juices."

We. Was Eli remembering his betrothal or thinking about workers? Perhaps he was not as self-seeking as his brother?

Abishua and Keenan's sandals scraped against the

stone steps leading to the base of the press. Her muscles relaxed, leaving her limp and slumped against the uncomfortable fitted rock. Eli had shown some cunning by coaxing his father away from her position.

Her mind whirled. If Eli wanted to claim this land, he could have made her presence known. His father would have demanded a wedding night. Such an occasion could produce an heir, and Eli's line would be selling wine for generations.

Why didn't Eli cause his family to stumble over her? Once he knew their visitors were not bloodthirsty Canaanites, he could have called out her name? Was this a test of her affections? Or his?

She cradled her knees to her chest and wrapped her arms tight around her legs. The breeze had cooled. How much longer would she have to wait? Did Abishua need a tour of the whole vineyard? Was Mahlah wondering about the delay of their return?

Something wiggled between her toes. Slick and hard was the night crawler. No spider was as firm bodied. Still, she spied the ground for kin to Eli's massive spider. Digging a finger between her toes, she dislodged a beetle. Quietly, she stomped the sole of her sandal over the dirt near her robe.

"Ready to stand?"

"Eli?" Her heart nearly scrambled away with the beetle. Cautiously, she stood, making sure her legs were able to bear weight. Her limbs ached and tingled at the same time. She stomped her foot again, but this time it wasn't to squish crawlers.

"Are you sure your father has left?" She squinted into the darkness for movement. The landscape of the valley was not familiar as of yet.

Eli leaned against the wall next to her, leaving a

proper distance.

"I made sure they were gone. I even waited unless they doubled back to see if I was alone."

Even Eli knew of his brother's craftiness.

She shuffled her sandal in the dirt and then met Eli's piercing one-eyed gaze.

"You could have alerted them to my presence, and we would be sitting in front of the elders of Manasseh." She said it. The truth. The doubts about Eli that caused her uncertainty.

"I've been slapped, beaten, and humiliated by elders recently." He dipped his head and beheld her with an intensity she had never faced before from a man. "I don't want men to insist I perform the duties of a husband while they parade outside of my tent. Somehow, I do not believe you would seek that attention either?"

"No. No, Eli. I would not." Her breaths hitched at the thought of such a scene. "Though, we must return—"

He slammed his fist into his palm. Even with only the moonlight bathing his face, she detected every crease in his shadowed features.

"Do you think I'm unwise to the timing of my father's visit? He brought Keenan to inspect our vineyard. Where was he in the heat of the day? I was here with Reuben and other elders." Eli paced back and forth, crunching stones underfoot.

She rubbed her arms to stay calm.

Eli loosened his clenched fist. "After leaving Shiloh, when I worked with Jeremiah, I saw more kinsmen showing respect to my mute brother than to me. Am I not older? Did I not fight for Manasseh?" His forehead furrowed. "Look at me. I fought bravely at the end. Forceful enough to lose my eye." He huffed. "Does that not mean anything? I drank to forget it all while my father forgot about me."

"Eli, you did what was right. For me, for us, for my sisters." She tried to halt tears from falling, but they wet her cheeks anyway.

"You were the calm sister." A slight grin relaxed his mouth. "The one who didn't make much noise. Who am I to burden you with more turmoil?"

Pushing away from the wall, she stepped closer to her betrothed. "I am no stranger to rumors or grief, yet I have always followed our God. And His laws." Full on, she met his stare and held it captive. "That will never change."

He nodded. Brief as it was, she would accept his agreement and remember it.

A slight breeze, thick with the scent of soil and fruit, refreshed her spirit. She glanced at the fields blanketed by onyx shadows. Working the land did not frighten her when she beheld its beauty beneath the stars. "I believe if we do our best to honor God with this vineyard, the God of Jacob will bless us."

"Even if we only fill one jug with wine?" He grinned with a downcast mouth.

She laughed. "Even if we only fill half a jug."

"Eli!" Reuben stalked toward her, lamp held high.

At the bark of her intended's name, Tirzah and Reuben's son Jonah fled from Reuben's wake and toward the clearing.

Milcah's hands trembled as if they held all the crawlers from this night.

"If my wife has her way, Eli, you may not be able to fill any vessels." Reuben's chest heaved.

Eli stuttered a reply.

She stepped toward her brother-in-law, heart hammering. "I am the owner of this vineyard, and I need my betrothed to fill many jars. Do not threaten his well-being or my future. Haven't you been acquainted with me long enough?"

Now, she was anything but the calm sister.

15

When had she ever had to defend her actions? She had older sisters. She had Mahlah's bold reasoning to divert scandal. Noah would grasp her whip and challenge any naysayer. Hoglah had a legendary temper and tongue. The fourth daughter of Zelophehad avoided trouble or perceived a way out of it before it began. Now she faced an elder who was married to her eldest sister and who was balking at her retort. Her reputation and that of her vineyard would be tied to Eli if he lived long enough for a ceremony. She would muster all her strength to cast off gossip and slander about Eli's actions. Her inheritance would prosper with a son of Abishua at her side.

Folding her arms in front of her chest, she beheld her brother-in-law. "Forgive our tardiness. We had decided to return when uninvited guests arrived. You may have seen them on the road."

"I saw no one." Reuben stomped closer to Eli. If her brother-in-law did not hold a lamp, she would have sworn sparks flew from his glare.

Eli cleared his throat. "My father and brother came to inspect the vineyard."

"Were you seen together?"

Eli shook his head. With his thumbnail, he scratched at the mortar in the grooves of the press. "Do you think me a fool?" He hesitated. "I hid her out of sight behind this stone wall."

"Abishua and Keenan took their time leaving." She scuffed her sandal over where she had crouched. Her heart pained for Eli. Their clansmen had long memories when it came to his misdeeds. "Surely, they have seen these vineyards before when you battled in the valley?"

Reuben rested the lamp on the wall. "Mahlah was afraid there was more to your delay. If you do not marry within the clan soon, she fears some clansmen may continue to challenge your ownership of the vineyard. She sent Tirzah and Jonah to stay the night here with you so no one would settle your land." Reuben's gaze switched from her face to Eli's and back again. "If Keenan did not scout this valley in war, he has seen its bounty tonight."

"Joshua gave me a year to marry." Did she desire a celebration straightaway? "What about Tirzah's wedding? Or the harvesting of the grapes?"

"This is Zelophehad's portion," Eli said. "It does not belong to anyone else but his daughters."

Eli's words emboldened her spirit, but her hands still trembled. She fisted them and tucked them close to her side in a self-embrace. Why did she wait to take a husband? Because it was Eli? Because everyone expected her to rush into a man's arms? Hanoch's ruby imprinted on the underside of her arm.

Wide-stanced, and apparently at a loss for reprimands or instruction, Reuben and Eli beheld her with befuddled expressions.

Lord, fill me with Your wisdom.

In the absence of raised voices, Tirzah tiptoed from the

other side of the press.

Good that Mahlah had sent two chaperones instead of one. Tirzah's and Jonah's abundant energy would come in handy when they searched the land for supplies.

Her own land. God had bestowed these lush fields on an orphaned girl. Why should she be hesitant to accept God's gift?

Turning toward Tirzah, she reached for her youngest sister. "I'm glad you have joined us." With a quick squeeze of her sister's hand, she beheld Eli. Then Reuben. Then the stars overhead.

"After the grape harvest, I believe Eli and I should have our wedding celebration."

"So soon?" Tirzah exclamation held a hint of enthusiasm.

"I'd do it sooner, but these grape clusters are about to burst."

Lunging forward, Eli knelt before her. "Are you sure?"

She wished she could deny any misgivings, but on this moonlit night, with Eli shorter than her height, she didn't spy a single crease on Eli's forehead or a lack of confidence in his features. Hope abounded. Hope that her future husband could manage a vineyard. Hope that her heart could receive love from another man. Hope that together, this vineyard would bring glory to God.

Jonah sprinted round the press. "Who's going to help stake the tents," he said, out of breath.

She tilted her head and beheld Eli's battle-scarred face. "See, we already have workers."

~*~

Later that night, Milcah rested on her side, head propped on her hand. Tirzah lay on her back on a bed mat. Sleep had not settled on their tent. Had Eli and Jonah found rest after Reuben left?

"The timing of my wedding does not bother you?" Milcah asked. Her youngest sister had been slated to wed Enid as soon as they settled in Canaan.

"Who says I won't be next?" Tirzah rolled onto her side. "You and Eli haven't harvested one grape."

"Tomorrow, we'll begin. Your feet are clean enough." Milcah sniffed the air loudly.

Tirzah laughed. "Enid thinks his cousins will be interested in working the winepress."

"Toda raba, Sister. We will have to figure out how to pay them. I could sell some of father's livestock. Noah would know which animals are mine."

Tirzah twisted her hair around a finger. "Sell some of Eli's livestock that he offered as a bride price. They aren't as healthy as ours, or,"—her whispers grew softer—"his cousins might wait until you sell some wine."

"If we sell some." Milcah's mind spun with the responsibilities set before her. "Let us hope our warriors did not discover all the riches hidden on this land." *Lord, may it be so.*

"Milcah." Jonah's rushed, raspy summons shrieked through the ramskin wall.

She scrambled to her feet, heart thumping.

"Someone is stealing your grapes."

16

Milcah flung on her cloak, grabbed the knife Eli had given her, and raced from the tent with Tirzah on her heels. Eli waited outside with a sword strapped on his hip.

How Jonah or Eli spied the pickers, Milcah didn't know. Darkness had covered the clearing like a thick burlap sack. Only the dominant moon gave light to the rows of grape vines except for a dim light fluttering far in the distance. If they did not confront the thieves, then their plants would be picked clean by pagans.

No more. After this night, word would travel throughout the valley, and throughout the city of Megiddo, that this land belonged to Zelophehad's daughter. Granddaughter of Hepher, and a descendant of Joseph, beloved son of Jacob and ruler of Egypt. Pilfering would not be tolerated in her fields anymore. The vineyard had a steward.

She hurried toward Eli. "You are not going alone into the fields."

He stiffened. Had she spoken like a battle commander? Breathing deep, she softened her demand. "We do not know how many there may be. Allow me to go with you. I have your gift and a loud voice."

"You do?" Tirzah frowned. "I've hardly heard you yell. Well, except for when we crossed the Jordan River on dry ground and the day Eli fell on you."

"I'll go with him." Jonah shuffled toward a donkey with as much enthusiasm as a turtle.

"No." Milcah held out her arm. "What would I say to Mahlah if harm came to you? This vineyard is my responsibility. I have to trust that God gave it to me for a reason." She rubbed the throb in her temples. "Jonah, you have to stay here and guard Tirzah. We have already welcomed male visitors this eve."

Eli tugged the donkey from its post. "This is insanity. I can handle a few fruit pickers. They will most likely flee when they hear the clop of the donkey."

She bit her lip, thinking. If the thieves fled, they would come back. She could not stay alert through the night, every night, waiting to ward off criminals.

"You're right." She jabbed a finger at Eli.

"Toda raba." He dipped his head and glimpsed their witnesses.

"About the noise the donkey's hooves will make. We need to prepare a surprise attack." She whirled and pointed at the rows of shadowed plants. "Can you count the rows to where you see the light? We will scale this hill and confront them before they realize the caretaker has arrived."

"They are seven rows in," Jonah announced proudly.

Eli huffed. "I have not agreed to this plan."

"But you think its best, right?" Tirzah came alongside her sister. "Soon, you will have workers to pay. You can't let robbers steal from your profits."

Shaking his head, Eli stomped toward the other donkeys. "I am only agreeing to this because I am sure of my swordsmanship." He slipped the bridle from his mount. "God would not bestow a vineyard and allow pagans to claim it by spilling Hebrew blood."

This was a demeanor from Eli that Milcah had rarely seen. If ever. He was assured, confident in himself, and confident in God. He had been wounded in battle, but he had escaped war with his life. Unlike… She tamped down her memories and focused on the trouble at hand.

Eli motioned for her to follow him.

"Jonah, keep watch." Eli's simmering growl had Jonah wide-eyed and nodding. "If anything seems amiss, take Tirzah and flee on the donkeys."

"Please," Milcah added. "I don't want harm to come to you." Her heart squeezed at the loss her family would suffer if Jonah and Tirzah perished.

"What about you?" Tirzah was chewing her fingernail as if it was Hoglah's bread. "What if they overpower Eli?"

"That could never happen." *Again.* She kissed her sister. "We are going forth with God."

"I was more comforted by our rallying cry when we had thousands of our tribesmen around us," Tirzah said.

"We still do, Sister." Milcah lifted her hands toward the stars. "These are the lands of Manasseh." She brought her hands together. "We should pray."

Eli stationed himself at her side. "Hear, O Israel."

They all joined in prayer.

"The Lord our God, the Lord is one. Love the Lord your God with all your heart and with all your soul and with all your strength."

"Praise God." Her gaze wandered toward Eli's muscular arms. She had no doubt God would protect her. And somehow, in the shadows of this night, she knew Eli would do the same.

She jogged after Eli as they descended a grassy

embankment leading to where the rows of grapes flourished. Her lungs burned from matching Eli's rapid pace. She snatched a robust grape to sweeten the sour taste on her tongue.

Traveling toward the road, they carefully counted the lines of grape plants until they had reached the seventh row. Eli tapped his sword and motioned for her to give him a berth to draw his weapon. He unsheathed his blade. Muted light gleamed on the worn iron.

From grape plant to grape plant, they slipped closer to the thieves. The width of the plants and bush-like thickness of the grape leaves and clusters, blocked their bodies from view.

Her palms dampened as they neared the pickers. She wished she had drunk her fill before hurrying into the field, for her tongue could not find a drop of saliva. Was Eli as frightened? Or did year upon year of battles, prepare one for a fight?

Eli stilled.

Branches rustled on the next planting.

With the stealth of a predator, Eli shifted into the middle of the path.

Someone ducked from under the grape leaves, basket in hand. A boy. Not much older than Jonah. Ten years of age at most.

The young man did not flee, or attack, or give a defense. He stared. Dropping his basket, he leapt backward and tripped, felled by the girth of the basket brimming with grape clusters.

"Where did you run off to, Yarrat," a woman's voice asked in a harsh whisper.

Suddenly, crawling from underneath the tall stalks of the plant, a babe appeared. A girl with cheeks darkened by Milcah's grapes. The girl's face crumpled. She collapsed onto the path and whimpered. Her round-eyed gaze fixated on Eli's sword.

These bandits were a family. Milcah's heart hollowed at the sight of the little girl's torn covering.

"Answer me, son." The woman ducked from the next row, tossed her grapes at a half-filled basket, and shrieked. A spooked lark catapulted toward the night sky.

The little girl wailed. The boy remained prone on the ground, feigning a corpse.

"Do—do not harm my children." The woman dropped to her knees. Her words and her clasped hands begged Eli to spare their lives.

Eli remained a sculpture of flesh.

"We mean you no harm."

Milcah approached and stood by Eli's side. "This vineyard was given to us by the One True God. It is an inheritance from my father."

The boy scrambled to his feet. Hands fisted, he yelled, "You killed my father."

Finally, the little thief had spoken.

17

Milcah opened her arms to the woman and her crying child and displayed empty, harmless palms. She and Eli had not meant to scare a mother and her children. Where was the victory in startling the vulnerable? Her heart squeezed as the woman's chest heaved. Milcah ignored the boy's insult. How could a pagan understand the power and plans of her God? At times, she did not understand them, but she remained faithful to the God of Abraham. The soil she and Eli trod was a gift, a spiritual inheritance, and she would honor God with this vineyard.

"My father is no more, as well." Milcah beheld the boy's snarled face. "It is through his death that I have become the caretaker of this vineyard."

"Yarrat. Hold your tongue," the woman rebuked her son in a broken dialect. She bowed her head. "Do not hurt my son. We will give you our harvest."

Eli scrubbed a hand through his wavy hair. "Do not fear. You are not in danger from us."

Milcah bent and placed scattered clusters into the woman's basket. The round, firm grapes were cool upon her fingers. "I will not challenge the Living God and his granting of this land." She shifted the basket closer to the mother's feet. "If you are a widow, then you and your children may glean from the edges of our fields. We will not harvest to the borders of our land. Our God watches over the widows, orphans, and the weak. I should know, I am also an orphan without a father." She glanced at the boy. The young man's gaze stayed intent on Eli's sword. His sister crawled to their mother.

Eli sheathed his blade. The leather muted the lethalness of the iron.

"Do not wander so far into the vineyard," Eli cautioned. "Our kinsmen may take offense at your presence. Though, we will do our best to keep you safe upon our land."

Our. Had Eli embraced his new lot in life?

The boy rose and brushed off his backside.

"We can come during the day?"

"Show your respect, Yarrat." The mother lifted her daughter from the dirt.

"Because he has a weapon?" Yarrat's brow did not unfurl.

"Because these men defeated the kings of Megiddo and Beth-Shan. Mind your tongue." The woman turned to Milcah. Her features devoid of purple stain, contrasted with her daughter's grape-mashed lips. "We are grateful for your provision. It is not always safe along the road." Bowing again, the woman rubbed wetness from her cheek onto her tattered robe.

Milcah remembered the man in the chariot who had followed her people's trek into the valley. The man did not show his face, but he made his presence known.

The girl twisted in her mother's arms and reached for Milcah. The girl's dark-lashed eyes reminded Milcah of Noah's daughter. Milcah's taut muscles became like cream.

"May I hold her?" Milcah held out her arms.

"She needs a wash. Her linen is soiled." The mother bounced her daughter. To no avail, the tiny arms still clawed for Milcah.

Milcah smiled. "I have many nieces and nephews. A younger, unmarried sister is called upon frequently for such a chore. It would be an honor to hold her."

The mother hesitated.

"I speak the truth."

Gradually, the mother released her babe into Milcah's arms. A faint odor of urine wafted from the girl's tiny tunic. A washing would be in order when Milcah returned to her tent. A washing for dirt and because she had touched unclean pagans.

The woman glanced between Milcah and Eli. "You are not married?"

Words to describe her closeness to Eli in the dark, and their rushed betrothal, vanished from her brain.

Eli cleared his throat. "We are to wed soon. After the harvest." Eli dipped his head toward his intended. "We came as one this night to protect the vineyard. We wanted to honor my wife's father, Zelophehad ben Hepher."

"We meant you no harm. By meeting under the stars, we have made an introduction. I am Zhirta and these are my children, Yarrat and Doti. Tomorrow, we will gather nearer the road."

Doti rested her curly, matted hair on Milcah's shoulder.

Zhirta gathered her basket and drew a waterskin closer to her harvest. The bulging waterskin could bathe Doti thrice over.

"Where did you draw your water?" Milcah asked. "In the city?" A water source nearby would save time for their workers.

"You do not know?" Yarrat jogged past Eli and a couple of grape plants. "A well stands where the fields flatten." He pointed to the north, jumping to indicate the location in the cover of night.

"We have a lot to learn about this land." Eli followed Yarrat and strained to glimpse the area.

Milcah carried Doti as the women strolled toward the border of the vineyard. Zhirta set her basket on the ground and received her limp and weary daughter.

"Praise the gods you were not seeking blood this night." Zhirta nodded and stroked her daughter's hair.

Sharp and stabbing, a pain shot through Milcah's body. Their befriended widow had blasphemed in God's field.

"Only the name of the One True God may be uttered in this vineyard." Milcah's correction came out bold. Bolder than any other reprimand she had bestowed. "No other name can be spoken." Milcah met Zhirta's gaze. "It is forbidden."

Yarrat came and stood beside his mother. "What about the goddess of the harvest?" He slipped the waterskin over his shoulder and lifted the basket round with fruit. "Asherah has fed us in the past."

"She will not help you now. Every god is a false god but the God of Abraham, Isaac, and Jacob." Milcah would not allow a single mouth to utter the name of a pagan god on her land. She crossed her arms over her belly and stomped her sandal. "As much as we have visited together this eve, if you align with a goddess, you are not welcome on this land."

"How will we remember the name of your God?" Yarrat's shoulders collapsed as if he carried a boulder instead of grapes. "The God of Abra…ahbrah… Abram?"

"We will try to remember," Zhirta scolded her son.

"The God of Abram will do." Eli strode and stood at the edge of their vineyard. "The men who conquered these cities were descendants of Abram." Eli indicated the city of Megiddo barely visible in the distance.

"Do you have a carving of him that I can put in my basket?" Yarrat asked.

Cheeks flaming, Milcah rubbed her sticky hands together. Doti did indeed need a bath.

"We do not make images of our God. He is alive, and His law does not allow it." Milcah caressed Doti's cheek. "Do you understand, Zhirta? Anyone caught with an idol with be thrown from this vineyard."

"I am trying to understand." Zhirta's eyes glistened with tears in the moonlight. "There is much to learn."

"Do you have a carving, son?" Eli's voice echoed in the darkness. He placed a rugged hand on the boy's shoulder.

Yarrat shook his head.

"Good." Milcah's heartbeat calmed. "You are a wise son. This bounty is a gift from the Creator."

"The God of Abram?" the mother answered.

Yarrat blew out a long breath. "I knew that name."

Milcah grinned. She bobbed her head in a show of understanding. "The God of Abraham. The One True God has blessed us with this fruit." She plucked a grape from a cluster dangling nearby and ate it.

The mother shivered and glanced at the road.

Were bandits about at this hour? Milcah squinted into the shadows. Or had the man in the chariot returned?

Eli stepped away from the road and hid in the branches and full foliage of a grape tree. His hand rested on his sword.

"May we sleep here until morning?" Zhirta licked her lips and snuggled her daughter. Yarrat moved alongside his mother, features stoic, eyes pleading for a blessing.

"You may stay," she and Eli said in unison.

Yarrat raised his chin toward the stars and closed his eyes. "Thanks be to the God of Abram." Opening his eyes, he grinned with an expanse of teeth.

She matched Yarrat's grin. She had stayed true to her God, and now a Canaanite uttered God's name in thanksgiving. It would have caused her a heavy heart to throw the widow and her children out of the vineyard and into the darkness.

"Peace be with you," Milcah said.

"And you." Zhirta hurried into the thick of the vines.

Eli, hand still perched near his blade, joined Milcah. "Let us return to the tents by way of the road."

"You are not afraid?" What if an elder happened upon them?

Eli stared at her as if she were a stranger—as though he had met her for the first time, stealing grapes.

"You are remembering a different son of Abishua."

He misunderstood. She should have made her words clear. She did not believe him to be a coward. Well, not of late.

Before she could explain her question, Yarrat raced after them.

Huffing, he said, "If you go to the well and find the storehouse, you may want to bring an ax."

She bobbed an acknowledgement of Yarrat's warning. "Thank you for informing us."

When she turned toward Eli, he had gone. Her intended was stomping away from her, farther down the road.

While her heart had softened this eve, another one had hardened.

18

She had defended her God before Canaanites yet offended her future husband. Calming her warrior winemaker would not be as easy as calming a sister. She had to convince Eli that she did not believe him to be frightened of chariots or bandits. She had asked about his worry with their reputations in mind. She needed him. In the morning, they had to start producing wine and so far, their workers were her sisters and a few children.

"Eli. Slow down." Her sandals *thapped* against the trampled ground as she rushed to catch her betrothed. "You did not give me time to explain my words."

He rounded on her. Loud breaths rushed from his chest. "You think me a coward?"

Now, who was the one frightened? She shook her head and loosened her covering. Linen hung down her back, freeing strands of her dark brown hair.

"I did not think of you as a coward." Her brow furrowed at his accusation. "I thought of you as a lover."

His good eye glistened in the moonlight. He drew even closer. Close enough that she could smell the earthy leather from his eye patch.

"I mean." She licked her lips. His eagle eye followed the arc of her tongue. Her heart became a battering ram upon her body. "Um, I meant, along the road we could be seen by an elder. Traveling together." She flapped her hand between them. His gaze still pierced her like a lance. At least he didn't have two eyes to behold her angst.

"Believe me. I would never insult you. Well, not now."

Still staring, he stayed motionless. His broad shoulders blocked her from being seen by any stragglers on the pathway.

"Not since our betrothal," she added.

He quirked a brow.

"Say something." She clasped her hands. "You know as well as I do that my sisters may have slandered you a time or—" She began counting in her head.

Eli laughed. "I believe you. How could I not. You have been honest with your words."

He strolled toward the edge of the vineyard and braced an arm on a branch thick with grape clusters. He plucked a grape and plopped it into his mouth. "My reputation has not always been praiseworthy." He loosened another grape and rolled it between his fingers. "I will do everything I can to bring honor to our union."

She sauntered closer, righting her head covering so as not to appear wanton.

"Truthfully, I did worry about our arrangement in the beginning. But now,"—she plucked a grape for herself to enjoy—"I'm hopeful." She bit down on the little round fruit and smiled. His features were shadowed and obscured by the hues of the night, but she had grown accustomed to the jut of his jaw and ridge of his cheekbones. Some may think his face a bit wild with his scars. To her, his healed wounds showed maturity and sacrifice.

As she reached for another grape, he reached for her. He folded her hand between his own. His flesh warmed her fingers. Under the branches of grapes, he commanded her attention. The press of his hold tightened against her ring. Hanoch's ring. Her memories faded. Eli and this vineyard were her future. Even the crickets were cheering Eli's closeness.

"We best return and calm any fears among your sister and your nephew. We will have work aplenty in the morning."

A caress, slight and soothing, traced the length of her thumb. Eli's daring touch had her prancing giddily in the winepress.

Her reply delayed in her throat. "Apparently, I have a well and a storehouse to assess." She dipped under an especially full branch and pulled him toward the road.

In no hurry, Eli followed, whistling at the blinking sky.

What had happened in their vineyard this night? She had convinced her intended that she did not believe him to be weak. And he had made her believe that burning his lily was a mistake. For under the vines and the branches, something began to bloom in her. Could she forget her past loves as Eli forgot about his past transgressions?

His whistling song silenced as they traipsed the small incline leading to the clearing by the winepress. Lamp light glowed near the tents.

"Praise be," Tirzah said. She sprung from her tent flap. "We saw the light move toward the road and then stop."

Jonah rubbed his eyes. "Did the thieves run or fight."

"Neither." She glanced at Eli. His caress still pulsed

upon her skin. "There was nothing to be frightened of in the vineyard. A mother and her children gathered food." She grasped Tirzah's hand and kissed it. "Our troubles begin when we start work at daylight."

19

The next morning, Tirzah elbowed Milcah's side. Her youngest sister balanced a water jar on her shoulder and pointed toward the road.

"Your workers are starting to arrive."

Milcah set her jug on the smoothed ground of the clearing and rushed to embrace her sisters.

Leading the procession was Mahlah. Her eldest sister tugged on a donkey that pulled a cart full of her children. Noah and Hoglah marched alongside the cart. Hoglah carried her niece, Miriam, while Noah coaxed the cart riders to stay inside the wooden slat walls.

Praise God for her family. And vineyard workers. But why had Hoglah come to the vineyard? Had she forgiven Eli for his youthful transgressions? Somehow Hoglah and Eli needed to bury the memories of the pagan pit in Peor and not allow the blunder to spoil the blessings from God.

Eli and Jonah left their stations where they cleaned the treading floor. They descended the stone steps to greet the early morning arrivals.

"I am praising God for my sisters and these empty baskets on the cart." Milcah snatched a basket and lifted

Abigail from the cart bed. Aaron lay swaddled by his older brother Amos.

Hoglah returned Miriam to her mother. Noah had her shoulder sling ready for the curly-haired little beauty.

"We can't let these grapes rot on the vine." Hoglah sauntered closer to the bottom pools of the winepress. "Besides, you told me I could make raisin cakes. With all the passersby on the road, I will make a small fortune selling olive oil and fruit." Hoglah cleared her throat. "I will need these same hands to harvest my olives, too."

Mahlah secured the donkey to a post not far from the press.

"We have plenty of hands to pick grapes, but we may need more baskets." Mahlah brushed off her robe. "I could spare only a few jars as well."

Where would she and Eli get the needed supplies to haul grapes and store wine? Her sisters could pick clusters, but who would stomp the grapes?

"Is Reuben bringing more workers?" Milcah asked. Even though the sun had yet to reach its full fury, sweat dripped along her hairline. She set her water jar next to Tirzah.

Mahlah draped an arm over her shoulder. The familiar waft of myrtle, their mother's favorite scent, calmed Milcah's nerves. Her family would not let her struggle in vain.

"Reuben and the other elders are hearing any grievances about land portions," Mahlah whispered.

Milcah stiffened. She grabbed hold of her sister's hand and kept Mahlah's warmth wrapped around her body. "My inheritance is safe, isn't it?"

Mahlah glanced toward the press, "Eli looks alive and well, and you look as satisfied as a landowner can be with much work to be done." She widened her eyes and tilted her head in Eli's direction. "Reuben told me about Abishua's visit. I am glad you stayed on your land so Keenan did not get an unhindered look around. May no one attempt to steal our father's rightful share."

"Praise God we have Reuben to plead our case," Milcah said.

"Remember, God decided our case. Abishua may be bold, but I do not believe him to be a fool." Mahlah squeezed Milcah tight and released her sister.

Tirzah let out a long sigh "Milcah and I were on our way to the former owner's storehouse. He may have jars and baskets hidden inside. It's by a well."

"Water?" Hoglah untied the donkey. "Take this cart and fill the skins. If I'm picking grapes, I'm not fetching water. Lamech is sending his cousins and their families to assist with the harvest. They will arrive later with Enid. We will need plenty of water for the heat of the day."

What if the storehouse was empty? She and Eli would have workers and no crates or baskets to ferry the clusters to the press.

"I pray the former winemaker has a bounty in his storehouse." Milcah reclaimed her water jar and placed it in the cart. "If not, we will have to go to the markets in Megiddo."

"Not without a man, you won't." Eli grabbed one of Mahlah's waterskins. "We need to finish cleaning the stones, and then we will be ready for large feet."

Tirzah laughed and wedged her water jar onto her hip. "Then it's a blessing Milcah and I are going into the vineyard. Our older sisters have bigger feet."

"Wait until you give birth, Sister." Noah picked a spindly branch from the clearing and chased Tirzah. Baby Miriam squealed with delight at her mother's antics. "Big feet are better than a big mouth."

"Is Basemath here? Look here she comes." Tirzah raced down a path next to the dividing hill while Noah turned to see an empty clearing.

"You tricked me," Noah called. "Wait until you return."

"Praise God for sisters." Milcah grinned and led the donkey and cart away from the press and in pursuit of her youngest sister.

Halting her run, Tirzah bent at the waist. "Which way is this well? I can't see over the plants. One row seems to blend in with the other."

Milcah veered the donkey toward where Yarrat had pointed. "We should find it on the other side of this section. It's not too far from the road. That's what the boy said."

"Did he mention it before or after you allowed his family to stay and harvest." Tirzah snapped a grape from its cluster. Drops of indigo juice stained her fingertips. "We could be wasting our time."

Yarrat had believed she and Eli knew about the well. Speaking falsely about it wouldn't further his family's interests.

"Keep moving. We'll be there soon enough."

Passing through a wide lane in the middle of the groves, Milcah glimpsed the faded brown boards of a storehouse.

"Over here, Sister." Milcah swerved southward. The donkey grazed on a few spiraling tendrils before following her lead.

Milcah progressed past the formation of grape plants into a clear-cut field similar to the wide-open space near the winepress. A planked storehouse stood not far from the last row of grapes. In the distance bathed in sunlight, the rounded stones of a well were visible. But it was the stripe, the thick, shadowed gray line that marred the stones, the grass, and the ground that caused Milcah to retreat from her warehouse.

"Is it full?" Tirzah asked, coming alongside her.

"The building is the least of my worries." Milcah squinted into the torment of the sun's rays. "I should have heeded Yarrat's warning."

Tirzah shaded her eyes and tilted her chin toward a carved wooden pole. "What is that?" She gripped Milcah's arm. "Who is that?"

Shivers chilled Milcah's skin. "The boy spoke of a goddess of the harvest."

"Well, with those plump breasts and burgeoning belly, I would say we found his goddess."

20

Milcah averted her eyes from the scandalous carving. Hadn't the warriors of Manasseh toppled these pagan idols when they conquered the land? How was this idol left standing? Tirzah had commented on the flourishing of the grape vines. With the wooden figure barely reaching the top branches, perhaps she was meant to be hidden. Truly, anyone venturing to this well or storehouse would see the wooden woman. Not so, someone marching past on the road. This insult to her God had to be removed.

"Someone's coming." Tirzah's face grew gaunt. "What if it's a worshiper?"

Parch-mouthed, Milcah whispered, "Run behind the storehouse. We will double back to our sisters." A high-pitched hum filled Milcah's ears. She pushed Tirzah toward the building. "Go."

The donkey trotted a few steps forward as they raced around the storehouse. They would catch the beast later. He was not wandering far with a cart attached to his sides.

Tirzah vice-gripped her arm as they waited flat-backed against the wooden planks of the building. Milcah's chest burned as she breathed. An aroma of freshly cut trees filled her senses. One thing was for sure, her vineyard had been well-kept.

"Milcah?" a man shouted.

Tirzah released Milcah's arm and allowed the blood to flow. "That's Eli. Why did he follow us?"

Was her sister casting dispersions on Eli? He had nothing to do with this idol.

Milcah's heart rate calmed. She emerged from the side of the storehouse and met her betrothed.

Eli gawked at the carved pole. He held up an ax.

"You forgot this. I remembered Yarrat's words after you had left." He turned as Tirzah joined them. "Looks as if we're going to need it."

"What do we do with her?" Milcah avoided gawking at the naked carving.

"Throw her down the well and be done with it," Tirzah said.

Eli scratched his chin. "I don't want any piece of that carving left on our land. I'll chop it down and we'll burn it."

"Out here? With all the trellises?"' Milcah made a mental note of where the greenery ended in relation to the idol.

Eli shook his head. "We can't risk a fire in the vineyard. We'll take the pieces back to the winepress and burn the wood in a fire pit. I will turn her to ash myself." He thrust the ax into the air. "And if anyone else wants to throw a piece in the flames, let them."

"Are we going to place the pieces of the goddess in the cart? Will it make our supplies unclean?" Milcah bit her thumbnail. The taste of pine sap made her mouth bitter.

"I'm not riding in the cart." Tirzah hugged herself. "This is the first time I wished we were back in Gilgal. Our sister almost died after she went into a pagan pit of worship."

"This isn't the same," Milcah assured her sister.

"Isn't it?" Tirzah glared at Eli. "He should know. He was there with Hoglah."

Milcah's mind spun with retorts, but a defense of her betrothed was lost in the tendrils that seemed to snake through her brain and snatch her words. Her mouth gaped, but all she muttered was a wisp of her sister's name.

"We are not worshiping this god." Eli's voice cracked as he spoke. "I will slay it with my ax, and we will destroy it by fire." Eli slammed the harmless side of the blade against his palm.

Tirzah shook her head, her lips a thin line of whitening flesh. "I will go in the storehouse with my sister, but if I see another carving of that woman, I am leaving this vineyard."

Milcah stood firm as a rock in the middle of a river with two streams battering its position.

If she had not switched portions with Tirzah, her youngest sister would be the owner of this vineyard and this pagan goddess.

Eli stalked toward the stout carving. "This is from the God of Abraham, Isaac, and Jacob." Eli braced his legs and swung the ax. *Whack.* Chips of wood sprayed from where the ax struck the idol. Again and again and again, Eli swung his weapon, vibrating the oak pole. His muscles bulged with each blow.

"Praise be," Milcah shouted. "We serve a Living God."

"Come, Sister." Tirzah stomped toward the storehouse. "I've had enough of this spectacle. You can open the storehouse door and scout if there are more idols inside."

Couldn't Tirzah see what was happening before her eyes? Eli was felling an idol. Did her sister doubt Eli's outrage? Milcah clenched her teeth lest she confront her sister and cause even more tension this day. The day of her first harvest. Eli's and her first harvest.

She traipsed after Tirzah and prayed no more foul images adorned their land.

Crack.

Milcah turned.

The voluptuous goddess tumbled and landed in the dirt.

Eli thumped his chest and raised his ax. "Now, I will cut her to pieces." His mane of hair bounced off his back with his first fatal strike.

Had she ever seen Eli in such a rage? He had allowed her to confront the suspected grape thieves in the dark, controlling his reservations. Her stature slumped. Why did this blessing from her father have to come with idols and tasks she had no idea how to fulfill?

"Hurry," Tirzah called. "We don't have all morning. Enid will arrive with his kin soon."

True. Her sister spoke with reason, but how could she ignore the destruction of a carving used for pagan worship. Eli was ridding God's Promised Land of an idol.

Milcah caught Eli's gaze as he raised his ax for another chop.

"Cut her small enough to fit into the cart. We don't want her nakedness recognizable by our workers."

Eli nodded and continued his labor with renewed vigor.

Hurrying toward her foot-tapping sister, Milcah stifled a smile. The man glistening with sweat in the morning's rays was nothing like the man ridiculed by their kin. *Praise be, Adonai.*

Using her shoulder, Milcah thrust open the door of the storehouse. Her sandals slid over wooden planks powdered with dust. Bits of pollen and dirt floated in the sunlit air. Her senses bathed in the aroma of pine and oakwood. Breathing in the stale air, she coughed.

Four large jars set in the farthest corner. The four corners of the building could have held forty more jars.

Tirzah fanned a hand in front of her face. "Looks, as if you will be traveling into the city for supplies."

"At least it's a start." Milcah grabbed the lip of the closest jar. "Why does such a vast vineyard have no wares?"

"Thieves." Tirzah gripped the other side of the jar. "You confronted some last night. I'm sure people have been pilfering anything they can sell. With all the travelers passing by on the road, your jars are probably on their way to Egypt."

"Undoubtedly so, for they are not here."

Her gold band clinked against the baked clay jar as she and Tirzah loaded the first vessel into the cart. Would Hanoch's gift buy enough supplies in Megiddo? Could she part with his ring?

The constant thumping of Eli's chore continued outside. Her future husband had acted honorably during their travels to the valley. He hadn't gotten drunk or left her with the work of cleaning the winepress. Her father's inheritance had bestowed a vineyard. She would see it succeed. Even so, a tiny part of her heart still ached when she remembered Hanoch. How would he have managed these fields of grapes?

By the time the waterskins were filled, Eli had piled all the chunks of the goddess into the cart. The Canaanites' wooden hope was cut to fill a fire pit.

On their return trip, Tirzah guided the donkey. Her

sister stayed as quiet and unresponsive as the tired beast. Why had Tirzah scratched open old wounds about Eli and Hoglah's foolishness? Both had imbibed and followed wayward elders into a worship pit for a false god. The offerings at the Tabernacle should have removed the memories of the incident.

Eli joined her as she followed the cart. Her four jars stayed upright, held in place by dense chunks of wood and hefty waterskins.

The aroma of an honest day's work wafted on the breeze.

Eli dipped his head to catch her attention. He grinned, but a shadow of shame quivered his lips. "One day I will have a name you can be proud of."

"I am proud of your labors." She let her voice carry to any plant or person who cared to listen. "Our God allows for atonement. Offerings were made for your and Hoglah's transgression in Peor. Mahlah saw to it. And so did your father."

"Hoglah is a fine woman." Eli swiped his hand along the hearty green leaves of the grape plants. "Lamech praises how she runs his household."

"Only a fool would criticize my middle sister. Lamech would be bones and skin if he didn't sing her praises." She beheld Eli's interest. "We all cause suffering at times."

"You?" He shook his head. "I don't believe you have ever stirred the ire of others."

She stifled her laugh so as not to irritate Tirzah. "I have four sisters," she whispered. "Ask them, and I'm sure you will find a fault."

"What if I don't want to?" His gaze struck her with an eye as rich in color as the purple grapes that flooded past her line of vision. Her insides twirled more than the thin yellow-green tendrils searching for a stalk.

Speechless. That's what he had rendered her. She looked to the harvesting that needed to be done. "We could work on improving my reflexes."

"We could."

She caught the curve of his mouth straightening.

Up the incline, the donkey jogged. Eli rushed to reinforce the station of their wine jars.

"Take the lead," Tirzah shouted. "Enid is waiting for me in the clearing."

Milcah rushed to aid her sister. The rope lead itched against her skin, but she cajoled the donkey over the last hump and onto the path by the hill.

A few men waited near the winepress. Wives and children picked grapes from nearby rows, their limestone and alabaster colored head coverings peeking out from the green and indigo lines covering the fields. Woven baskets overflowed with grape clusters. Lamech and Enid's kin would need to start treading soon.

Tirzah's hands were all a flutter. No doubt, she had recounted to Enid their shocking find near the well.

Nearer the road, at the edge of the clearing, Hoglah bent over a rock. She rolled the stone to complete a circle. When she saw the cart, Hoglah's fist perched at her hip.

"We need to feed all these workers before their feet are washed with grape juice."

Why did past sins have to taint her sister's name this day? Hoglah may grumble, her complaints may always be ample, but she made the tent of Zelophehad's daughters a home. No one's cooking fire smelled as fragrant as Hoglah's.

Eli marched past, dragging the donkey that balked at his pace. His aim was toward the circle of stones and her sister. His stride quickened as he drew near. Unless Hoglah intended to sprint down the hill into the first line of trellised grapes, no escape existed from Eli's charge.

Heat prickled upon Milcah's cheeks. Why was her betrothed confronting Hoglah?

"Wife of Lamech." Eli's voice carried in the open space. "We have a chore to do together. I bring a special kindling for your fire."

Hoglah's gaze snapped around like a hungry chicken searching for seed. Her husband and another man jogged toward the cart.

Eli clapped his hands and held them toward the cloudless sky.

"Today, on the vineyard belonging to my wife and her father, we felled the carving of a false god." Eli grabbed hold of the cart's wooden slats. "Many years ago, I led Hoglah astray. Into forbidden fields. We were young and followed leaders who caused us shame. Death settled on our camp. This day"—Eli turned and addressed a small crowd that included Mahlah and Noah, who had appeared from the vines–"We will throw a false god into the fire and rid Zelophehad's land from this evil."

Strolling closer to Hoglah, Eli held out a log of wood. "Will you join me, Sister? Let us start a fire with this pagan pole and forget my foolishness. May God grant us peace in this new land."

Hoglah glanced at her husband. Lamech gave a slight nod. One by one, Hoglah met her sisters' gazes. Her mouth opened and closed, but no reply came forth.

Tears pooled in Milcah's eyes. Would her sister accept Eli's offer and banish the harsh memory of Peor?

Hoglah strutted toward the cart. Her hips swayed as she rounded the donkey's muzzle. She took her time as if inspecting goods from a tedious merchant.

"What took you so long, Brother? I could have had bread baked by now if you had brought me this wood sooner. Now I am behind plucking grapes for raisins." Hoglah lifted a chunk of wood. "Blessed be the daughters and sons of Jacob." She tossed the wood in the center of her cooking pit. "Who has a lamp? Do not tell me we don't have a flame." She tilted her head at Eli. "Don't stand there; I am waiting for our fire."

Eli bowed and hurried off toward the press.

How had finding a pagan pole turned into an offering of peace? Milcah swept a tear from her lashes and gazed at the green hill separating her land from Tirzah's. Wind blew across her face, cooling her cheeks. *God, who am I to receive such blessing?*

Hoglah and Eli unloaded the cart, tossing chunks of scandalous wood into the crackling orange flames. Clouds of gray smoke billowed and fattened as the cart emptied of its contents. Sisters, grape pickers, and winepress workers backed away from the scorch of the blaze. Curious children were kept safe from Hoglah's raging fire pit.

Higher and higher the flames rose. Bits of ash drifted over the clearing.

No blaze burned hotter than the warmth engulfing Milcah's heart. Eli had offered Hoglah peace from the haunts of her past. Would Hoglah's forgiveness set him free from the burdens he carried?

Milcah couldn't brush the wetness from her face fast enough. Something was taking root in her heart that she had banished after Hanoch's death. She cared. She needed. She desired. *Lord, do not take another husband from me.*

Noah comforted her with a snug embrace.

Where was baby Miriam?

Chest heaving, she glimpsed her niece in Eli's arms. Miriam's tiny hands grasped at his eye patch. Her betrothed threw back his head and laughed. Miriam was undeterred in her quest to possess her uncle's leather covering. Of course, she would be; she was the daughter of Noah, granddaughter of a man who raised five daughters.

Milcah pressed her lips together and reclaimed her composure. "It's time to make some wine." Releasing a suppressed laugh, she added, "And raisins."

21

With night settling over the valley, Milcah leaned against the winepress to relieve her aching muscles. Eli stationed large lamps around the clearing. Lamech's kinsmen staked tents at the end of the sloping hill. A few men harvested still, with lamplight. Tirzah had abandoned the vineyard to sleep in Mahlah's tent. Her youngest sister refused to cut any more grape clusters. Lamech's aunt would stay in the tent tonight. Milcah doubted the older woman would snuggle close and whisper about weddings and hopes. A single tent no longer sequestered the snores of the daughters of Zelophehad. She should have been praising God every day for that bygone blessing. Soon, her future would join with Eli, and they would share a tent. How soon she did not know.

Her insides churned in a whirlpool at the thought. She traced the mortar bonding the winepress stones. Muted purple grape skins floated on top of the juice stomped on the treading floor. The vigorous cutting of clusters had filled the circular walls more than halfway. Loaded bins overflowing with grapes waited to be crushed. Where would they put all this juice? If only this vineyard had come with a winemaker.

She swallowed the thought. A Canaanite overseer would worship the false goddess they had struck down earlier in the day. This was God's land now. Given to her tribe of Manasseh.

Eli leaned over the wall, balancing his weight on his arms.

"We trampled a lot of grapes."

"We did?" She grinned at his weary face. "Our kinsmen did." She tugged on one of the ropes dangling from the crossbeam. "These ropes kept our workers from falling. Unlike a certain man I encountered."

Eli laughed heartily. His robust chuckle sounded like foreign babble. Had he ever dismissed his folly so easily?

"I'm glad you can laugh," Milcah said. "You have worked hard today. Cutting down an idol. Harvesting grapes. The men listened to your instruction on the treading floor."

"Any owner would have done the same." He tapped his sandal against a burgeoning crate.

"Not every winemaker would have included my sister in the destruction of that hideous carving." She dipped to capture his full attention. "Toda raba."

"You are to be my wife." Eli rubbed his hand on the stone rim of the press. "Hoglah and I need to look to the future. Not the past. Didn't her husband arrange for laborers?"

"He did." Leaving a few crates between them, she inspected the open pool of juice. "I hope they return tomorrow to stomp again."

"Hah!" came a high-pitched rebuke.

Eli whirled, hand on his blade.

She turned and scanned the clearing. The glow from the lamps did not reveal an intruder.

"Leave the grapes be." Yarrat rose from the incline. A tattered waterskin hung from his hand. "You need to poke them with a stick."

Eli scowled. "How about I poke you with a stick. What are you doing prowling around our vineyard?"

Our. Her heart warmed at the bond strengthening between them.

Milcah sauntered toward the boy, her fright waning. Hadn't he warned them about the false god? Indirectly?

"You seem to know a lot about this vineyard. You knew where the idol stood." She gave Yarrat her best older sister stare and crossed her arms against her chest.

"You found her?" Yarrat inched closer.

"And chopped her into logs," Eli said. "She heated our bread."

"Oh." The boy's lips pressed thin. "Do you have any waterskins that need filling? Ours is useless." He held up the busted skin and rubbed his bare foot along the ground. "My sister is thirsty."

Her bones ached at Yarrat's admission. What would it be like to live in a godless land with no king or protector? She didn't want to find out.

She grabbed a skin from beside the winepress. "I will trade you. My skin for yours. If,"—she glanced at Eli and nodded—"if you tell us what you saw the winemaker do with his crushed grapes."

Yarrat scrambled closer. "You need a stick to poke the grape skins into the juice. Poke them for a few days."

"A few days." Eli scrubbed a hand over his hair. "Some of the grapes are shriveling on the vine."

"You came too late." Yarrat waved his hand as if their coming was within their control. "Sell some of the grapes along the road. Isn't there a woman making raisins?"

"How long have you been lying in the grass?" She

held up the bulging waterskin to tempt the truth.

Yarrat assessed the trade. "Not long. Voices carry in the fields." He shrugged. "I saw a woman sorting grapes this afternoon."

Truly. Several people heard Hoglah's complaining.

Milcah continued to enhance her standing. "The jars in the storehouse. Where did they go?"

Eyes wide and glistening in the lamplight, Yarrat shrugged. His interest in the skin's abundant water faded. "Storehouse?"

"By the well." She tamped down her frustration with the elusive boy. "We only found four jars."

"They are worth something. Many people scrounge for wares. They sell them for food." Yarrat reached for her waterskin. "Can I get some water for my sister?"

Visions of little Doti whimpering for a drink flooded Milcah's mind. She handed Yarrat a full waterskin.

"You have helped us with your knowledge. See that your sister drinks her fill."

The boy accepted the skin, bowed, and fled down the hill into the rows of grapevines.

Eli came and stood beside her. He retrieved Yarrat's tattered skin.

"I believe that boy is hiding some truth?"

"He has given us guidance." Milcah wrapped her head covering tighter around her neck. "Perhaps God is answering my prayer in an unusual way."

"With Yarrat?"

She stifled a smile at her husband's shock. "I prayed we would have a prosperous vineyard, and a young Canaanite is the one sharing his wisdom. Who can predict what God will do? And with whom?" Would she have thought Eli and Hoglah would have made peace over burning a goddess of the harvest?

"His waterskin was full the other night." Holding Yarrat's burst waterskin, Eli ran a finger over the ripped bladder. "This has been slashed with a knife."

"It can't be Yarrat's fault." Milcah inspected the tear. "Why would a boy destroy his family's waterskin?"

"Perhaps he didn't."

Milcah pressed a hand to her heart. "No one mentioned a fight in the fields. Truly, we would have heard the shouting if someone attacked Yarrat or Zhirta? We had workers in many rows."

Eli glanced across the vineyard toward Megiddo. "What if the assault didn't happen here, but in the city?" Eli quirked his brow. "I need to find more jars before the next treading."

"We need to find more jars." She tried to fight it, but deep inside her spirit, she heard the whispers of her tribespeople. The gossip that said she was cursed. That Eli would join her other suitors in the grave. She twisted her gold band. By habit. A habit she would need to break. "If you venture into the city, I am joining you. I need to know the market and the merchants, too." *In case you are not long on this earth with me.*

Silence.

Was Eli remembering the whispers, too?

He tossed Yarrat's waterskin in the ashes of the fire pit and strode to where Yarrat had emerged. Eli lifted a long branch from the grass of the hill.

Had Yarrat brought them the wooden pole?

"I can submerge the grape skins with this stick," Eli said. He returned and swirled the vat of juice. The night air grew tangy with the aroma of trampled fruit. "That boy better not be filling our heads with foolishness."

Milcah tapped her foot lightly. "We will know when we go to Megiddo in search of jars." And answers. "Truly, if thieves stole those large vessels, they will want to sell them to us for a price." Though, what would they give for a trade?

Lamech's aunt emerged from Milcah's tent. "Don't you sleep, girl?"

Not when her future was tied to this vineyard and to Eli.

22

A long, steep, curvy road led into Megiddo. Milcah rested with Tirzah in the back of a second wagon following Eli's wagon into the conquered city. Travelers halted on the side of the dusty entryway and let their small caravan pass. As the sun reigned overhead, sweat pooled above Milcah's lip. Was it the heat or the trepidation for what they would find inside the walls of the city?

Squeak. Squeak. Squeak. The wooden wheels protested the upward climb. The clop of donkey hooves slowed. Lamech and his cousin guided their wagon closer to impressive walls the color of soured milk. Oh, how they contrasted with the ribbed green fields in the valley. Above the stone entry, a carving had been hacked flat in some areas and in other areas, burned.

"Will Eli turn back if there is trouble?" Tirzah's knuckles matched the pale of Megiddo's stones.

Milcah pulled a basket closer and nibbled on the grape clusters.

"Eli and Lamech fought here. Our fighting men settling in this valley killed their king and slayed his army. These people have more of a right to fear us than we do to fear them. Their king and their gods are dead."

Tirzah glanced at the gateless entryway. "At least they can't keep us prisoner."

Milcah reached for her sister. "We are here to find jars. Not to begin a battle."

"Good. Because I hope to marry soon. Enid is asking about a time."

"We should celebrate soon." Milcah let her voice sing. "All this change and travel has come when you desire to be settled with Enid." She tossed a grape at her sister. "We must talk to Mahlah."

"It is so good to hear you say such." Tirzah's eyes sparkled in the sunlight. "I love being a sister, but I want to be a wife, too."

"So shall we all be." Except she had the elders minding the time when she had to take a husband.

Behind the gate, a large, open marketplace greeted visitors. Defeat in war had not tempered the fervor of Megiddo's merchants. Men shouted at the wagons with wares raised high. A man rushed forward holding a sandal in each hand. He danced in a circle. Did Eli and Lamech appear wealthy?

Not to be out sold, a woman jogged beside the wagon bed tossing bits of spice into the air. Her gibberish may have been unclear, but her cumin and garlic enriched the breeze. Hoglah used the same bold seasoning to flavor her meals.

Glancing toward the entrance to the city, Milcah's muscles knotted. A chariot with a grand animal at its front waited near the stone archway. Was it owned by the same man who followed her family into the valley? She would have sworn she heard chariot wheels the night she met Yarrat sneaking her grapes. She shook her head. Truly, several Canaanites traveled in this manner.

Eli settled his wagon on the far side of the marketplace near a trough. Some wise merchant had placed the trough opposite the entry, so visitors had to travel the gauntlet of booths and tables in order to water their livestock. A few goats nuzzled the wooden slats placed to hold Eli's jars upright. Her betrothed did not have much livestock left to trade. Lamech stationed his wagon beside Eli's. He and his cousin could water the donkeys and goats while Eli searched out jars.

Her betrothed approached. "Bring the baskets of grapes. I will inquire about jars for storage." Eli strolled toward the closest booth.

Before Milcah could balance her basket of grapes on her hip, women gathered round her and Tirzah. Some reached at the clusters with bony fingers. They clutched coins barely larger than a plump raisin. Hoglah would have no problem selling her cakes in the city.

Eager, or desperate, the women pushed closer. A barterer held a coin in front of Milcah's face. The image of a false god scowled from the bronze.

Milcah's cheeks burned hotter than a bad sunburn. "Do not take their coins, Tirzah. Not if there is a false god etched onto them."

"There are so many hands." Tirzah's back pressed against Milcah's. "How will I know?"

Milcah held her basket over her head. "Do not pay with images of your gods. We serve the One True God."

"We need jars." Tirzah slapped at an overzealous woman. "Didn't you hear? Jars."

On tiptoe, Milcah cast a glance and saw Eli engaged in a brisk conversation with a merchant.

Hurry.

Milcah shook her head covering and flailed her arm like one of Tirzah's tantrums.

"Bring us jars or something to trade."

A full-faced woman with a brightly embroidered robe pushed to the front of the raucous crowd.

"I have what you seek. Come." The woman smiled with teeth as thick as a mosaic tile. "Over here." She waved for Milcah and Tirzah to follow.

With Tirzah clutched to her clothing, Milcah dodged scurrying children and dipped past wide turbans toward a table loaded with sandals, pouches, and leather bracelets designed like the ones Noah wore.

Their impressive shiny-haired leader whisked back a curtain and displayed three tall vessels identical to the ones in the storehouse. This woman or her husband had ventured outside of the city and traipsed across the vineyard.

Before Milcah could ask the price, a shriek rose above the din of the marketplace.

"Let me go." A young boy scuffled with a man clad in leather greaves and wearing a similarly designed breastplate. Had the man recently purchased items at this booth?

She knew that haughty whine. Truly, it was Yarrat.

"I don't know where it is." The boy flung his fists in defiance.

Milcah nodded to the grinning merchant and held up her hand. No one else seemed interested in buying the jars, and she could not ignore Yarrat's distress. The boy may not be an Israelite, but he had given some assistance to her and Eli, little as it may have been.

"Where are you going?" Tirzah stayed molded to the table.

"Our night visitor is here." Milcah rushed forward. "The boy is in trouble."

"That thief?" Tirzah said.

Pushing through oblivious merchants, Milcah came upon the tower of a man striking Yarrat with his leather boots. The foreigner's feet rammed Yarrat's ribs. The boy rolled in the dirt attempting to avoid another kick.

"No," Zhirta screamed. "Stop." Doti cried, cradled in her mother's arms, the girl's nose was a well of water.

How could she turn a blind eye like these foreigners? A boy and his widowed mother were being tormented by a scoundrel.

Milcah took the deepest breath possible. "Leave him be!" Her command turned the heads of engaged merchants.

The leather-clad warrior glared her direction. His face was hidden by cowhide tooled with an ornate design. All she could see were his eyes. Onyx orbs as lifeless as a corpse. A scallop of thin leather shaded his mouth.

Inside, every inch of her quivered, but Milcah would not be deterred. Not by this pagan.

"Don't harm the boy." Her throat flamed with every word. "He is a worker in my vineyard."

A growl of a laugh rumbled from the intimidating foreigner. He perched his leathered foot on Yarrat's stomach.

A belch bubbled from Yarrat's mouth.

"You are a woman." The warrior sounded as if he had a mouth packed with linen. "Who are you that you could order me to do anything?"

The raspy shout of the masked heathen halted sales in nearby booths. Buyers and sellers stared her direction, shaking their heads in a quiet warning. She would not flee and leave the barterers to believe her people were cowards. Megiddo's king had been slain by the sons of Jacob.

"I am the owner of a vineyard." She held her basket of

grapes high. "This family harvests in my fields." The assailant didn't need to know they gleaned instead of receiving wages. "If you harm the boy, you owe me for his lack of labor. Do not touch him further." She roared louder and longer than she had ever done in her life. Longer than her scream when Eli plunged on top of her. Louder than in any fight between her sisters. And louder than any rant of Hoglah's.

Yarrat's attacker stilled. He didn't move a muscle. His foot remained planted on her young thief.

Her skin chilled in the heat of the sun, but she did not glance away from the leather-covered man's penetrating stare.

He released pressure, sending Yarrat scurrying toward his mother. The boy stationed himself in front of Doti, chest heaving.

With his hand gnarled into a claw, the fighter lunged her direction.

She hurled her basket of grapes at his frightful face. The woven container thumped against his leather-clad chest. Clusters of grapes scattered in the air and fell toward the market's dirt floor. Women dove to collect the fruit. Their bent bodies were a sea of camel humps between her and the warrior.

"Do not harm my workers. And do not step foot on my land." Milcah's heart skittered so fast, she coughed to slow the beat. A salty taste like death settled on her tongue. "The One True God protects the orphan and the widow."

A cool shade bathed her shoulder.

She whirled and beheld Eli. Head tipped, his unpatched eye beseeched an answer to her shouting.

His ruddy-cheeked presence was a balm to her pimpled flesh.

"What has upset you?" He glanced at the ground. A few unclaimed grapes rolled in the dirt. His forehead grooved. "Did you fall?"

"Fall? That man attacked Yarrat." She pointed to where her enemy had stood tormenting their acquaintance.

The warrior had vanished.

Casting a glance to where Zhirta and Doti hovered, she saw nothing. No one crouched in fear. No one lingered to explain the confrontation. The mother's hiding place was empty.

Milcah rounded on her sister. "Tell him Tirzah. You saw the boy? That man?"

"Briefly." Tirzah shrugged. "I heard someone screaming, and then you yelled. I went to get Eli."

Around, all around, merchants, buyers, heathens, and wide-eyed children gawked at her. Bold seasonings, body odor, and the sour stench of sunbaked hides accosted her senses. The commotion in the marketplace became a pestering hum. She knew one thing. This chaotic city would never be her home.

Eli cleared his throat. "The sun is hot here on the hill. Would you like some water?"

She nodded. Her throat had started to burn.

Eli accompanied her and Tirzah to a station of watering jars.

And of course, under the stone archway, the chariot was gone. The warrior had wanted something from Yarrat. Was the boy hiding a secret? If he was, why did she believe it was connected to her land?

After a few sips of water, she asked, "Will we be going home with jars?"

Eli's expression was more frightening than that of her enemy warrior.

23

Milcah didn't believe the trip into Megiddo could get any worse. The relentless sun scorched the linen atop her hair. The people's coins held the image of a false god. And an armed man had attacked a boy in her midst. Now, Eli's features drooped in defeat. She would not leave this city without jars for her vineyard.

"The woman at the far booth has jars similar to the ones found in our storehouse." She casually indicated the big-toothed woman. "She may have more."

"They do." The admission did not buoy Eli's spirits.

Tirzah stopped sipping her drink. "Why are we waiting? I do not want to spend any more time here."

"Neither do I." Milcah scanned the travelers and barterers for a leather-clad fighter.

"Neither do we." Lamech and his cousin lounged against Megiddo's wall.

"The woman's husband can fill both our wagons," Eli said loud enough for his companions to hear.

That was good news. Though, Eli fidgeted like Yarrat.

"What is the price?" she asked.

"More than the goats we brought." Eli's jaw flared.

"And he will not accept a trade in knives."

Tirzah let out a loud breath. "Can't he wait for your wine? He can see the fields from here."

"No." Her refusal came out a bit harsh. "I will not be in debt to a pagan. Our wine is not ready, and I doubt he will accept grape juice." Milcah's finger itched beneath Hanoch's gift. The gold band effortlessly circled her damp fingers.

Her mind searched for possessions of value. She had a portion of her father's livestock, but the animals bred and supplied her with offerings, milk, and a future. She had Hanoch's gift. What would her ruby fetch?

Slipping the gold from her finger, she discreetly held it in front of Eli so as not to draw attention from bandits. The faceted ruby sparkled like a noblewoman's gem.

"How many wagons full of jars will this ring purchase?"

Tirzah gasped and gripped her arm. Her sister's basket lay abandoned by the water jar. "What are you doing, Milcah?"

Eli stepped closer. His broad frame would keep their treasure a secret.

"The ring is beautiful, but I cannot ask you to part with it. I will think of something to trade."

"We don't have anything else." Milcah held the ring so it was almost touching Eli's hand. "We have to pay our workers with what we have left."

Tirzah pulled her away from Eli, toward the sand-colored bricks of the city wall and the squawks of competing merchants.

"You cannot give that ring to a pagan. Do you want that boastful wife to wear Hanoch's gift?" Her sister's whispered rant grew louder. "It is a betrayal of Hanoch."

Tears stung Milcah's eyes. "Keep your voice down. I

would never betray Hanoch, and I never have." Milcah tugged her arm from Tirzah's hold. "I will always remember Hanoch in my heart. How could I forget him? But I have Eli to consider and father's inheritance. I believe Hanoch would have wanted what is best for my future. We…Eli and I…we need jars."

"Don't do this for Eli." Tirzah's jovial face furrowed.

"I'm doing this for me and for father's name."

Tirzah held out her hand. "Give it to me."

"Do you have tall vessels that will hold gallons of wine? Will you sell jewelry from Enid, the man who is to be your husband?" Milcah willed herself not to sob. A rhythmic pulse beat at the back of her eyes. She had to bury her grief. Like before. Twice before. "Eli needs this vineyard, too. He is a third son trying to improve his reputation."

Tirzah dismissed her confession with a flip of her hand. "He fought all over Canaan."

"True, but he bears the scars for all to see when he did not battle well." Milcah held out her fist, the gold and ruby secure in her palm. "I can do this. For my inheritance." A tear trailed over her lip. The sting of salt couldn't compare with the pain of loss of a loved one. "Hanoch would understand." She forced a smile, shaky as it was. "You want to marry soon. I cannot keep my sisters working every day in the fields. Our juice needs to be stored."

Tirzah nodded, her head jerking as her own tears flowed. "Forgive me, Sister. Here I am impatient and casting dispersions on your offer. I want to marry, but then so did you. You did not get the chance. You have been desiring a husband longer than I have. You mourned. And endured much heartache."

Milcah drew her sister into an embrace. "You have been there with me through it all. Listening to my sobs.

Trying to cheer my heart. You, who laid beside me every night and caressed my back. Where would I be without my sisters?"

Tirzah wiped her eyes. "I believe if Enid was in need, I would offer my ring. Father would have been proud of the vineyard. Of all our lands." Tirzah's narrow shoulders sagged. "He would have sold jewelry for the jars."

"I loved Hanoch," she whispered into Tirzah's ear. "He is gone. I have another betrothed, and we are working toward a future. I need to do this on my own. For myself."

Tirzah hugged her tight. "I love you."

"I love you, as well." After a brief squeeze, Milcah stepped away from the familiar scent of myrtle and soap. She wiped her face free of tears. "How do I look?"

"Like me, I fear." Tirzah laughed. "As if we've been crying."

"Let us blame the sun and the height of this city." Milcah took a deep breath, turned, and strolled toward Eli. She did not want to grieve anymore. She held the ring in the sunshine. "Take this gold and make sure that merchant fills our wagons."

Eli dipped his head and held her gaze, his deep brown eye intent on her tear-stained cheeks. "Are you certain?"

"I have never been more sure of myself in all of my life." She handed him the ring, but she did not glance at the sparkle or at the glimmer of past hopes. The scarlet ruby was a reminder of the piece of her heavy, heavy heart that cherished the memories of a man she once loved.

She threw her shoulders back and smiled, weakly, but with a certainty of future. Her ring was such a small trinket in Eli's large palm. "We have more grapes to tread. Let us be on our way. Our clansmen will wonder where their winemakers have gone."

Her betrothed stood, beholding her. The merchant

shouted something in his foreign dialect, but Eli did not respond. Eli clenched the ring tight and shook his fist with her ring safe inside his hand.

"You will not regret this." Eye downcast, he turned with a purpose and marched toward the impatient seller.

Blessed. She was blessed with land and a vineyard. She reminded herself that her bauble was nothing compared to the gift God had bestowed upon her sisters. And spending the day in this market had made her grateful to serve the One True God.

Tirzah grasped her hand. "Lamech and his cousin can help Eli load the wagons. Save your strength for fieldwork. I will help Hoglah with the cooking."

"You will?" Milcah tried to make her words sound encouraging. "Aren't you going to sleep in Mahlah's tent tonight?"

"I'm going to lay in wait for your thief. If I stay with Mahlah, I will not be able to walk without a child underfoot."

"I will keep watch with you." Milcah tugged Tirzah toward the wagons. "That boy has more to tell us. He owes me the truth since I feed his belly with grapes."

Eli's goats, her ring, and Tirzah's coins filled Lamech's wagon with wine vessels. The jars sat tight against the higher wooden slats. Some of Eli's wagon was left bare, so Milcah and Tirzah stretched their legs in the back of the bed and braced any jar intent on falling.

After leaving the city, Lamech and his cousin started their donkeys down the sloping hill first. Milcah squinted at the wagon bed, making sure her jars did not topple or clink or crack. Praise God for a full load.

When they reached the road and turned toward the vineyard, movement caught Milcah's attention. On the slope, a chariot raced away from Megiddo. Dust stormed into the air clouding the pathway to the city.

Her cheeks flushed, but not from the heat; that was the least of her worries.

"Eli, she shouted. "That warrior from the marketplace is chasing us."

Eli slowed the donkeys. He turned and glanced over their load of jars.

"Do you know it to be him?"

"He is the only one I know with a chariot." And he was the only man she had insulted.

Tirzah worried her lip. "Maybe he will turn and go the other direction?"

"We don't have time to wait," Eli shouted to Lamech. The boom of his voice had the donkey's heads bucking. She, too, felt a fright in Eli's urgency.

Lamech slowed his wagon.

Eli motioned toward the city. "Send me your cousin and take the women. We have a fighter looking for another battle."

Lamech's cousin leapt from his seat and secured his sword.

Tirzah shuffled off the wagon bed and ran toward Lamech.

Milcah rose and jogged toward Eli.

"I'm not going anywhere, she said. "That pagan is looking for me. Get that full load of jars to the vineyard." She pointed at Lamech. "Hurry on. Gather some kin at the press."

"You cannot stay." Eli's snarled face reminded her of the panther that stalked Enid's livestock. Eli's eye grew bigger than a harvest moon.

"Yes, I can stay. This wagon will block most of the road."

"Milcah!" he shrieked.

Folding her arms, she fought the tiny girl inside of her that would run at the first sound of her father's rants. She fought the wounded girl whose loves died before she could say farewell. She fought the innocent girl who found Eli's bold side rather unnerving.

"I'm staying." Her blood seemed to pool at her feet. "I trust you Eli. This pagan is no match for you, a warrior from Manasseh."

Had she ever rendered a man speechless?

The next scream was Eli's. But it wasn't aimed at her. He ordered his kin about.

Lamech's cousin instantly blockaded most of the road with the wagon and then unhooked the mules.

The clan of Hepher prepared for another fight.

24

Eli hefted the jars out of the wagon and laid them on the road and in the dirt like fallen fighting men. Milcah rolled a vessel and finished their clay barricade. Yarrat's attacker would not shatter all her wares. Truly, she hoped the warrior was after her goods and not her life. Nor Eli's life. *Lord, protect Eli and our clansman. May we return to our vineyard unharmed.*

The chariot turned onto the road and progressed toward their crude fortress. The leather-clad pagan was no fool. If he charged their outpost, his horse would be lamed or wounded. His beast could not jump their wagon or the mosaic of jars, not with a chariot's weight at its tail. A grove of oak trees set a natural barrier at the side of the road where Lamech's cousin hovered, sword drawn. Their stalker could swerve to the far side of the path, but in doing so, he gave his enemies time to adjust their positions.

Milcah said another prayer and then swallowed, her throat clacking louder than the approaching chariot wheels.

Eli urged her to take cover in the oaks.

She neared the closest tree. "Aren't you embedding with us?" Losing another betrothed was unthinkable. She needed Eli alive to keep her inheritance, and she needed him to produce an heir.

Eli's gaze lanced the mysterious traveler. "He won't charge the wagon. Killing his horse would leave him on foot. We have him outnumbered."

"But what if he has a sling?" She should have asked Tirzah for her strip of leather and her pouch of rocks. Milcah's skills with a sling were almost laughable, but she would defend Eli and her kin.

"The wagon will give me cover. These slats hide my body." He grunted a laugh. "You act as if I've never been to war."

"I don't want you hurt." The truth in that statement gave her heart courage.

"We conquered this valley." He glimpsed her by her oak outpost. "We will do it again if we have to."

The chariot driver stopped. He stared. At Eli. Only Eli. *Lord, shield my intended.*

Her enemy turned and beheld her with snarled lips.

Was he mocking her? Or the One True God? Or both?

Eli sidestepped from the wooden lattice, staying near enough to the wagon for a dive. "Why do you threaten a man and his wife?"

A gurgling chuckle arose from the stranger.

"Your wife threatened me."

Heat hotter than a blacksmith's forge surged through her body. How dare this pagan accuse her of wrong-doing. She stepped from the protection of the oak's trunk.

"Only a coward harms a child. I defended a boy. One of the weak. The law of our God requires it."

The warrior flinched and clawed his rein-holding hand into a fist. He spat over the side of his chariot. "And which of the gods do you serve?"

Eli pointed his sword at the stalker. "We serve the One True God. He has given us this land. We conquered Megiddo and hung your king from the city gate."

"He was not my king." Defiance hissed from his masked face. "I bow to no god or man. They bow to me."

"Blasphemer." Milcah gasped, covering her mouth. Who would boast in receiving worship like God? The grapes she had tasted in the wagon burned the back of her throat.

"We—" she began.

"We bow only to the God of Abraham, Isaac, and Jacob." Eli and her clansman held their swords high. "Return to the city or come down from your chariot and fight."

She shivered at the thought of battle. Their adversary was a crafty foe. Why did Eli have to challenge him?

Laughter, again, chortled from the chariot.

"Why fight me and lose your chance to be rich among men. Bow low to me, and I will bring you workers. Merchants will scuffle to taste your wine." He held out his arms as if welcoming a brother. "Your plants will flourish without rain."

"Silence," Eli shouted.

Eli's rebuke of their assailant bolstered her courage and softened her heart. Truly, there had been a time when Eli might have assessed the pagan's offer. That time had ceased, so it seemed.

She stormed from the grove to address the mocker of her God.

"The lands of my father will flourish by the sweat of my people and by the blessing of my God. Your lies are an insult to our God. The Creator of this valley."

A distant clamoring of hooves drew her attention. She

glanced at the road behind her. Lamech had summoned their clansmen.

"Toda raba, Adonai." Her whisper stung her parched lips.

Snap. The crack of the pagan's leather reins echoed over the vast landscape.

The amber colored horse balked at its abuse. Yarrat's attacker turned his chariot in the direction of Megiddo.

"You know where to seek me."

Without a flinch or a show of concern that he may be struck from behind, the stalker left. He did not rush or flee in earnest. Why wasn't he fearful of a well-placed arrow?

"Do not show your face on our lands." Eli gripped the slats of the wagon bed. His body emptied of breath as if blowing into a flute. "You are a stench to my nostrils."

She rushed toward the wagon.

"You challenged our foe? All alone on the road."

"Are we ever alone?" Eli questioned her with words similar to what Mahlah would have spoken. Oddly, she could hear herself encouraging one of her sisters with his utterance.

"No, we are not." Milcah cast a glance at the slow-moving chariot and then beheld her brother-in-law and Enid slowing the charge of their mounts. "Eli." She voiced his name with reverence and with a boldness for his victory over the warrior. The man she had known years ago may have fled the fight. This man had defended her life, their union, and their God.

She cleared her arid throat. "When we return to the vineyard, I believe we should plan our wedding."

His mouth gaped then closed tight without an acceptance or a denial.

Clasping her hands, Milcah rocked forward and bestowed a glorious smile on her brave intended. "And may the celebration be soon."

25

A few days had passed since the threat from her pagan foe. Eli worked hard ferrying the jarred juice to the storehouse. To her knowledge, no preparations had been made to hurry their wedding week. She stirred the second press of grapes with her pole, submerging the grape skins that dared float to the top. Her muscles burned from reaching to the center of the winepress. How had Jonah managed this task for hours on end? She prayed her nephew would help with the harvest next year.

A vibrant orange sunset cast elegant shadows over the mountain fortress of Megiddo. Her nerves spun tight at the thought of traveling to the city again. Memories of her encounter with the warrior would best be forgotten until her next venture into the city.

Eli trudged toward her. The empty bed of the wagon gave her no concern. Jars had been filled, sealed, and settled in the storehouse. Why the former winemaker hadn't built the storehouse closer to the press, she did not know. Hemmed in by the hill on one side and fields on the other, the press stood in as good a spot as any. A wide, cleared path traveled the distance of the hill and then veered west toward the well and storage building. She forced herself to banish from her mind the image of the sculpted pagan pole.

"You are working too hard." Eli halted a few feet from her perch on the stone steps leading to the treading floor.

"We have more grapes to press. The sooner we jar this lot, the sooner we can stomp the waiting grapes." She loosened her aching-knuckle grip on the pole. Talking about a common purpose lessened her frustration about Eli's apparent hesitation to wed.

Eli scratched his stubbled chin and beheld her as if assessing his next task.

"I believe it would be best if our labor was finished before we have our days in the tent." He cocked his head as if to tease. "I can't have a bride fretting over our grapes."

She stilled and leaned against the pole, gawking. The potent aroma of ripe, mashed grapes almost made her faint and topple into the press.

"I've talked to Reuben and Mahlah," Eli said. "Enid and Tirzah as well. We settled on a single feast."

Her heartbeat boomed louder with each new revelation.

"No one dared to ask Hoglah to prepare food for two feasts." He stood as a man who had grown accustomed to these fields. To the work. And to a lifetime of harvests.

He grinned into the graying night. "You did suggest—"

"Yes. Yes, I did." Her words tumbled forthright. She couldn't bear to hear him repeat her offer. She had been bold. Perhaps, a bit afraid. Afraid Eli might die. Afraid of the gossip. The whispers about curses. Fearful of the elders snatching her vineyard. God's vineyard. As the evening air cooled, her body became a baking oven. "You are right to avoid Hoglah's wrath."

Eli grinned. His teeth gleamed white against his sun-bronzed features. "I knew her wrath well."

A shuffling of feet interrupted a sisterly response. She turned toward the fields.

Zhirta approached with Doti asleep on her shoulder. The mother's unhindered hand pushed her son forward.

Praise God. The widow and her children had escaped from the city.

"We come to thank you for your protection. Forgive us for not staying to speak with you." Tears cascaded down Zhirta's cheeks. "I am sorry. My heart was too scared. For my children."

Milcah laid her pole on the wall of the press and hurried down the stone steps.

"It is good to see you." The greeting tugged at her throat. "I worried you had been hurt."

Zhirta's lips pressed together. She nodded. "We have come to stay in the vineyard. I have brought some food with us."

If the food Zhirta had brought was in her satchel, the amount was too small to feed a family.

Eli left the donkeys hitched to the wagon. "You are welcome to settle on the edges of our land." His playful tone sharpened. "As long as our laws are followed."

The widow clamped a hand on her son's shoulder. The boy winced.

"We are...I am in your debt." Yarrat's gaze roamed between his mother and Eli. "I didn't mean to cause trouble."

How different Yarrat seemed from the first night when he was ready to pounce like a hungry predator.

"You were on the ground with a man's boot on your belly." Milcah tried to banish the image from her mind.

"Truly, you were not the assailant."

Yarrat rubbed his mid-section as if recalling the attack.

Now was the time, if any, to interrogate this curious boy. Hands folded across her chest, she sauntered forward. Some intimidation she wished to impart, but not enough to frighten their guest.

"The night we met you in our vineyard, Yarrat," —she met his shifting gaze—"you mentioned the pole and the location of the well. The man in the city wanted to know something. What did he question you about?"

Silence.

"Yarrat," Zhirta snapped. Doti snuggled deeper into the crook of her mother's neck.

The boy threw up his hands. He looked as thin as her stirring stick.

"He says I know where the king's wine was taken, but I don't." Yarrat pleaded with Eli. "I did not work in the vineyard. I would never be chosen to work for a king."

"This is true," Zhirta said with urgency. "We came into the vineyard when the king had died. When his men were no more. There was no one to stop us, and we were hungry and thirsty."

Eli drew closer to the boy. "You weren't the only ones in these fields. I bought the king's jars in the marketplace. Anything of value would have been stolen by now."

"We do not know what he is after." Zhirta glanced toward the road. "Only a few men worked this land. My son has scouted these fields, but he has not found any riches."

Zhirta and her children wore threadbare clothes and struggled to feed themselves. If there were treasures hidden among the grapes, no doubt Yarrat would have stumbled upon them, and his family would be dressed in finer robes.

"Was the man in the chariot loyal to the king?" Milcah asked. "Is that why he passes by my fields often?"

The mother shrugged as best she could with a daughter weighing her down. "He came after the battle with the Hebrews. He attends the sacrifices." Zhirta's eyes widened. "I do not go near the fires, but his chariot is there. I have seen it. Some say he is a…" her mouth shut tight.

Milcah appreciated Zhirta's restraint.

"There is only the One True God. Our God has given us victory in war. He parted the Jordan for us to walk across to these lands."

Yarrat strained his neck and stared at Eli's eye patch. "What does your God look like? Did he lead you into battle?"

Eli laughed. "I have not seen our God except as a pillar of fire at night and as a cloud during the sunlight. But He has told our commanders how to fight and when to attack our enemies. I followed a man named Joshua, son of Nun, into war. Joshua does not look much different than me."

Yarrat's nose wrinkled.

"Joshua has two good eyes," Eli said, masking a grin.

Her betrothed's banter with Yarrat encouraged Milcah's heart. When had she ever heard Eli jest about losing an eye? Her intended had gained confidence since they came to the vineyard.

"We do not mean to keep you from your duties." Zhirta nodded toward the press and dipped her head. "I am grateful for your protection. And the protection of your God. I do not know another that fights for the weak."

"And I know Him very well." Milcah acknowledged the woman with a tilt of her chin. "May we all have peace. Shalom."

Zhirta spoke to her son in a strange dialect. Yarrat followed her toward the edge of the field, closer to the road that led to the sea and the city.

As the sun disappeared behind the distant mountains, Milcah could not make out the family's trek between the lines of bushy grape leaves.

Tears pulsed behind her eyes. "Toda raba, Adonai," she whispered. What would have become of her sisters had God not bestowed protection and land to orphaned girls? A gust of night air lifted her head covering. She wrapped her arm about her waist.

Eli shuffled closer but not too close. He scanned the clear-cut expanse that led to the press.

"Tirzah and her companion, Enid's aunt, have returned. I will mind the winepress."

Milcah turned. Tirzah waved from atop her donkey. Jonah rode on a colt with a lamp for light.

Eli met her gaze with unease. "I do not want you to be fearful of that warrior."

With darkness covering them like a well-woven blanket, she asked a question to which she did not know if she desired an answer. "Eli," she hesitated, knowing that speaking the name of a sorcerer would bring a reaction. A reaction that would not be filled with the bliss and anticipation of their wedding. "Do you remember Balaam son of Beor?"

26

"Why would you utter such a name?" Eli thrust his head backward. His eye patch blended into the night. "I toppled that pole from the field and chopped an idol to bits. Your sister and I banished the memory of that night when we burned the goddess."

Tirzah stopped beside her. "Oh, I don't believe you are discussing our celebration." Her gaze locked with Milcah's. "I'll see you in a little while." Her mouth pulled to the side. She shuffled toward where the tents for sleeping were staked.

Enid and Lamech's aunt waited near the press.

"I am not toiling into the night. Come to sleep." The older woman crossed her arms and stomped a sandal.

"At least one of my nephews had sense to choose a reverent daughter."

Milcah's hands tingled. "I am speaking to my betrothed about an important subject. You may listen or retire. I have tasks to complete before I sleep."

"Well, if your father was alive, he would not hear a decent report from me."

Rounding on the woman, Milcah bowed slightly. "If

my father were alive, I would not be responsible for this vineyard."

Jonah lifted the pole from the winepress wall. "Isn't anyone tending these skins?"

"No," she and Eli chorused.

Aghast, the aunt backstepped toward the tents.

"Do not give anyone reason to cast doubt on our Tirzah. I will poke my head from the flap on occasion."

Milcah bowed toward the older woman. "I will retire soon enough." When had she become the sister whom women believed to be too bold? Hadn't her clansmen cast her as meek?

She returned her attention to Eli and paid no notice to her nephew stirring the juices.

"Perhaps you should sleep." Eli's tone sharpened. "You did not go to the pits of pagan worship with me."

Surveying the landscape of shadowed hills and the distant lights from the city and sky, she rolled her shoulders and cocked her head.

"But I saw Balaam. I was near him. He stood the distance Jonah is from us right now. Noah's goat was in his hands. He had stolen a nursing mother."

Eli did not challenge her recollection, so she continued.

"I screamed when I saw him, and as if he conjured the wind from his fingertips, a dust storm blew around Mahlah and me. He left the goat on the ground, tied with ropes and suffering."

Eli kicked at a rock near his sandal. "Why bring this up tonight?"

Swallowing, she considered what to share with her intended and what to leave in her heart.

"The man in Megiddo. The warrior who stalked us." She tried to twist Hanoch's ring, but her fingertips met only flesh. "That man makes me feel the same dread as when I glimpsed Balaam with our mother goat. Blood had caked in Balaam's big toe. In the ridge around the nail. Blood not from our goat." She rubbed her arm to calm the unease creeping over her skin. Her mouth was as dry as the desert. "Balaam was not only against us, Eli. He was against our God. I fear this warrior not only despises us, but he despises our God."

Eli stepped closer. Too close.

"I am not in a tent in Gilgal with my sisters anymore," Milcah said. "In camp, my kinsmen were all around me. I cannot see our house of worship." She blew out a shuddering breath. "I wanted my land and my inheritance. Though, now, my people do not live a few footsteps away from my tent flap."

"Jonah," Eli called. "Run to the road and see if my donkey is tied there."

A guttural acquiescence disturbed the clearing. Her nephew jogged down the wide path toward the road.

Eli, all of him, his broad chest, his rugged jaw line, all of his being, engulfed her body.

His gaze made her tremble. Not from fear, but with a wanting to be loved by a man. She had felt this want before, the warmth and flutter. She had fluttered until she mourned.

"You did not tie a donkey by the road." Her words were a wisp.

"Is Tirzah's future aunt peeking from the flap," he asked. His hand hovered a hair's width from her cheek.

She shook her head. "I don't believe so." Her swallow stuck in her throat.

"Do not fear when you are with me, woman. I have dealt with these Canaanites before. We are God's people. No false god or its sorcerer can stand against our God.

And soon, we will make more of God's people.

Before she could rise and see if Tirzah's aunt was truly asleep, Eli's lips met her cheek. His mouth was soft and warm like his breath.

All worry fled from her thoughts. Worry over a warrior. Worry about this new land. Worry over the son of Abishua who once wandered into a pit in Peor.

Her spirit soared to the sliver of moon that watched her intended's kiss.

Cautiously, briefly, she caressed his hand. "When do we wed?"

Eli captured another soft kiss. "Soon."

27

After the Sabbath, only a few crates of grapes remained to be crushed. The storehouse had little room left for the last of the wine. Hoglah had taken clusters to her land to bake in the sun and dry into raisins. Some cakes had been made from the initial harvest. All of Hoglah's delicacies sold rapidly to travelers journeying east. Milcah longed for the company of her sisters. Laboring in fields and feeding workers had stolen her days.

Before the sun heated the soil, she traipsed to the well to fill waterskins. She had risen before Tirzah and Lamech's aunt. A few of Lamech's cousins would arrive soon enough to finish the pressing. Then, when her vineyard rested from producing its fruit, she would become Eli's wife, fully.

Hefting the skins over her shoulder, she hurried along the path toward the sloped hill bordering her winepress. The weight of the water caused her to bend forward and count her steps. Oh, why didn't she bring a cart?

The circular stone press stood empty, alone, without men washing their feet and waiting to trod the grapes. Even Eli had vanished. A hint of worry took root in her temples.

Releasing the skins and laying them against the stones of the press, she squinted toward the road. Was the warrior taunting the downtrodden? Had he come to retaliate for her interference in the city?

A pack of donkeys trotted closer to her land. They veered into the clearing. Were elders arriving to check the status of her betrothal?

The rider of the lead animal waved. Waved enthusiastically.

"They've arrived," Tirzah said. She rested her chin on Milcah's shoulder. "Forgive me for not helping you with the water. Eli wanted to surprise you, and I wanted to sleep."

"Surprise me?" Milcah waved and then turned toward her younger sister. "Are my sisters carrying gifts?"

Tirzah laughed. "They've come to stomp the last of the grapes. Eli was concerned about you. He believes this vineyard needs to feel more like camp. Like when we were together in Gilgal."

"He said as such?" Milcah's heart squeezed. "I might have worried him. We spoke of Balaam and of the warrior who followed us out of the city. How one reminds me of the other. I don't feel as safe as when we were in Gilgal."

"Let that pagan come, and I will place a rock in his skull." Tirzah patted her sling.

"If only he was alone in his worship of foreign gods." Milcah shook her head and reached for Tirzah. "Come. This is a day of celebration. My sisters are all together."

Milcah sprinted toward her sisters. "I can't believe you're here."

Leaping from her mount, Mahlah embraced her sister. "I should have kept you in my tent until the harvest was over."

"No." Milcah held onto the warmth of her eldest sister for a few moments longer. "I would not have learned about the fields and about Eli. He is not the man I thought I knew."

Mahlah pulled back and smiled. "For that, I am glad you were here among the vines."

Noah strutted forward, tugging her and Mahlah's rides. "My brother-in-law better be treating you well. Jeremiah was quite forceful with him." Noah rubbed her knuckles. "And my husband will be again if Eli strays."

Milcah kissed her shepherdess's cheek. "I am grateful for you and Jeremiah. Eli's other brothers do not seem to care if he falters." Milcah stepped back and opened her arms. "Where is Miriam. I haven't been this close to you since she has been slung across your chest."

"Your future husband is helping tend the flocks and his niece. I do not know which he will find more challenging. You know, we have the most stubborn of ox."

"Yes, and my husband will hear from his aunt that we are slacking from our duties if those grapes are not crushed." Hoglah approached and motioned toward the tent. "I pray she sleeps a while more."

Dismissing the comment with a flap of her hand, Mahlah said, "Milcah's sisters are here to oversee the pressing of grapes. What slander can come of such a simple task?"

"Then let us hurry." Hoglah ambled toward the press. "You have water. Where are the basins for our feet?"

"I will get them." Tirzah ran and moved the wide wooden bowls closer to the steps.

One by one by one, the daughters of Zelophehad removed their sandals, cleaned their feet, looped their skirts into their belts, and jumped from the edge of the wall into the grapes.

Hoglah's nose scrunched. "These grapes feel slippery on my soles." She reached and grabbed a rope dangling from the wooden beam overhead.

"You have to take command of the grapes," Tirzah said, hopping side to side. "I've seen the men do this." Tirzah lapped around her sisters with a high-kneed waddle.

Noah threw her head back and laughed. "If I knew I would see you bare-legged and dancing in this sludge, I would have come sooner. Only a press can keep you contained."

Mahlah swung from side to side, elbows out. "I have wider hips than any of you. I can juice this fruit in one lap."

Milcah's spirit blossomed with petal after petal of love. Oh, how she had missed the banter of her sisters. She should have appreciated this gift more.

"Stop swirling through these grapes." Hoglah gripped the side of the press and held her stomach.

Tirzah continued circling. "When will we get to do this again? I will have responsibilities as Enid's wife next year." Tirzah swung her leg with enthusiasm. A grape skin flung in the air and stuck on Hoglah's cheek.

Tirzah slowed her prancing.

Hoglah bent and swept some mashed grape skins from the top of the froth. The grape on her face fell below.

"Now, sisters," Mahlah said, stepping in front of Hoglah. "We are helping Milcah with her vineyard. We must act as proper winemakers."

Splat.

Wet skins splattered on Mahlah's cheek.

Truly, it had to be Noah. Milcah turned.

Noah reared backward with laughter. Her wavy curls escaped from her head covering. "You are our eldest sister, not the manager of the vineyard."

"Why can't I be an overseer?" Mahlah dipped her toes in the mashed grapes and launched a mess at Noah. Grape skins struck Noah's neck and slithered between her breasts. "Maybe Jeremiah can find those later."

Mouth gaping, Noah fisted the nearest grapes.

"Sisters." Milcah leapt in between her two oldest sisters. "We are here to make wine."

Thump. Thump. Clump.

Wet fruit pulp slid down Milcah's cheeks. A rogue skin settled in her ear. She shivered at the slickness.

"Always ordering us around." Tirzah burrowed behind Hoglah. "I am so tired of picking grapes." Their youngest sister jostled Hoglah as a shield.

"Truly, stop," Hoglah said, ducking a poorly aimed mass of pulp. "I don't feel well."

"Are you dizzy?" Milcah waded to where Hoglah and Tirzah grouped along the press wall.

"No," Hoglah said with a swallow. "My stomach is unsure."

Tirzah slipped away from their middle sister. "Has anyone taken ill in the fields?"

"Everyone stay still." Hoglah clamped her eyes shut. "Or I may vomit in this wine."

Mahlah waded over. "When was the last time you laid with your husband." Her whisper entered every listening ear.

"Sister," Hoglah snapped. "Tirzah and Milcah are here."

Noah joined their intimate circle. "Our youngest sisters are about to go into wedding tents of their own. We shouldn't spare their ears."

"Mine are open and ready to listen," Tirzah said.

Milcah met her sisters' gazes, and they all laughed. All

but Tirzah.

"What? I can listen." Tirzah folded her arms.

Milcah enfolded Mahlah and Hoglah in an embrace. "I have missed sharing secrets late at night."

"This is daylight." Hoglah rubbed her belly.

"And you haven't answered Mahlah's question?" Milcah's plumped her sticky cheeks into a grin. "If you are with child, you would feel this way."

"It's been too long." Tears glistened in Hoglah's eyes. "I have petitioned God for years, and no child has come. Why should I be with child now? I am tired of hoping only to bleed every month."

Milcah grasped Hoglah's hand. Her sister's palm felt cool and damp. "We are settled. And we have received father's land." Left buried in her heart was the truth that her sister had made peace with Eli and with God over her past in Peor. "Mahlah may be right."

"You truly believe?" Hoglah blinked in the sunlight.

"I truly believe." Mahlah cast a glowing smile.

"I truly believe," Noah said. "Your aim was off."

Milcah kissed Hoglah. "Let us get you off of this treading floor." She led Hoglah toward the stone steps. "Later, you can tell Tirzah and me what to do with a husband."

Hoglah turned a deeper shade of trodden grape.

On the first step, Milcah halted. The flush of her cheeks drained to her toes. In the middle of the road, the pagan warrior waited with his chariot underfoot. He glared in the direction of the press.

"Why are you stopping," Hoglah said. "I don't trust my stomach."

"That pagan warrior has returned." Milcah descended the steps as if in a trance.

"The one who threatened you and Eli." Mahlah

strained to see the road from inside the press.

Noah waded toward Mahlah. "He has caused problems since he followed us into this valley. Even now he is gawking at married women with their unwed sisters nearby." Noah and Mahlah exchanged a look Milcah had seem all her life. A raised eyebrow look that followed their father's outbursts. A look that followed repeated slander of their sisters. A look that meant more gossip was forthcoming.

"Did you bring your whip, Noah?" Mahlah scaled the press wall with the determination of an ornery bull.

Noah bounded over the stones. "Always. You never know when you're going to meet a predator."

28

Milcah scrambled down the steps careful not to slip. Her feet slapped the stones, sending droplets of juice into the air. Mahlah and Noah followed her and released their hems from their belts. Noah uncoiled her whip and let it thud on the ground. Mahlah removed her blade from its sheath.

Were her sisters going to war with the pagan? Milcah's heartbeat echoed in her ears. She didn't want to mourn the loss of a sister. Her heart had ached and remained bruised for months after word of Hanoch's death. Even now, a slight pang needled her heart at his loss.

"I'll get my sling." Tirzah flew past her en route to the tent.

Isn't that where her own dagger from Eli lay?

"Wait for me," she yelled after Tirzah.

Lamech's aunt emerged from the tent. "What is all this screaming? I can't get any rest in this vineyard." The woman shaded her eyes. "Where are those women going on those donkeys? I can see their ankles."

"The man who threatened me is back," Milcah said,

sidling by the woman. "My sisters are going to ward him off our land."

Tirzah ducked past their clanswoman.

Lamech's aunt blocked Tirzah's path. "Shouldn't you wait for your husbands?"

"Have you ever met Noah's wrath. I fear her more than any husband." Milcah ran after her older sisters with Tirzah not far behind.

Hoglah had barely reached the end of the sloping hill while Mahlah and Noah were almost at the road.

The idol worshiper waited in his chariot.

Why did this fertile valley have to house Canaanites? She tilted her head back. "Lord protect Your servants. Go forth before my sisters."

Tirzah sprinted alongside Milcah. Strands of her dark brown hair blew in the breeze.

Milcah turned her head to the side and conjured a breath as she ran. "What did you tell Enid's aunt?"

"That she could rebuke me, but right now,"—Tirzah swallowed—"one of my sisters has a knife and the other a whip." Tirzah pointed toward the road. "I'm going to stand on that rock. I can launch a stone easily from there and strike anything in the open. If I can't hit that pagan, I will startle his horse." Tirzah veered toward the boulder.

Hoglah lagged, but she waved Milcah onward. "I will make it in due time." She dipped slowly to pick up a stick. "Why didn't father give me a weapon? I don't even have my cooking stone."

Father hadn't given Milcah a blade either. Eli had been the one to make sure she could defend herself. What would her intended say if he was here and not moving herds? She would deal with his displeasure later.

Mahlah perched high on her donkey, knife pointed at the pagan. Noah had ditched her mount and stationed herself nearer the front of the chariot. Hand raised, Noah dangled her lethal ribbon of leather and readied to strike.

Standing with her sisters before a masked fighter, Milcah relaxed as if this was the most natural of occurrences. The sun beat down on her brow and on her nose, but she would not let the heat bother her. This was what her sisters had always done. They had fought for each other. What could this warrior do? Could he shout louder than the men in the assembly who lamented their petition for land? Would he snarl and snap like a diseased panther? Was he greater than the sorcerer Balaam whom Mahlah insulted and slapped? God had always watched over the daughters of Zelophehad. The God of orphans had brought them into this land and blessed them mightily. The God of Abraham would not abandon his children now.

Mahlah twisted her knife in the air. The blade reflected sunlight onto the oiled leather of their foe.

"You have threatened my sister in front of witnesses." Mahlah's voice boomed like a commander demanding a surrender. "This very day, you have taunted my family. You are an enemy to the tribe of Manasseh. Do not show your face around our lands."

Tirzah whirled her sling. The rotating shadow warred with the reflection off Mahlah's blade.

Motionless as a corpse, the man observed her sisters. His soulless eyes never strayed from Mahlah.

Crack! The tapered tip of Noah's weapon struck the dirt not far from their enemy. The warrior's horse bucked and fought to retreat.

Milcah praised God for her sisters. These were the women who raised her to be bold for God.

"You heard my sister." Milcah strolled toward Yarrat's attacker. "You are not a Manassite. God did not bestow this land on you. We have fought to claim our inheritance. And we will not stop fighting until the name of our God is sung in this valley."

Snap. Noah flexed her whip again.

Whoop. Tirzah readied to let her rock loose.

Mahlah dropped her weight and prepared to lunge.

A wheeze of a breath came from the pagan's nose.

Hoglah shoved past Mahlah.

"I might be carrying the only child I will ever bear. If you come near my sisters, I will scratch out your eyes and eat them like grapes."

Milcah stifled a gasp. Her stomach churned as she pictured Hoglah's words. The middle daughter of Zelophehad had definitely strayed from her cooking fire.

Fist clamped tight around Eli's gift, Milcah raised her blade.

"We are the clan of Hepher," she shouted, pounding her bare feet against the pebble-ridden dirt. She chanted her clan's name again. Louder. So loud, she tasted the salty tang of blood. "We are the clan of Hepher, and we serve the One True God."

Zhirta and a few women shuffled from the last row of grape plants. They clutched their cutting knives. Their voices joined the chorus praising the God of Jacob.

"Depart," Mahlah yelled. "Do not show your leather-covered face on this stretch of land. My husband is an elder, and we will bring the swords of our tribe against you until you rot beneath this dirt."

The pagan's teeth bit into his lip, but he did not utter a sound.

Milcah met the warrior's gaze. It was not unfamiliar, but it still chilled her bones. The sing-song of voices quieted. She stepped closer to the chariot. Fear did not rule her. Her sisters would keep her safe.

"I do not know what you seek, but it is best forgotten. Anything of value found on this land will be given to our God." Her voice warbled, some. She swallowed and wished she had partaken of the water she fetched earlier. "I think it's best to heed my sister's warning."

Without a glance toward the city, or to where the road dipped, the pagan clapped his reins. His horse trotted toward Megiddo as if the mountain fortress was its barn and slings and whips did not threaten its coat.

Five orphaned sisters had won another battle. Praise God.

"Now, I really think I'm going to vomit." Hoglah blew out a long breath.

Her sisters met in an embrace with their weapons still clutched for good measure. Lamech's aunt approached with a stunned expression. No scold emanated from her pursed lips.

Held tight against the grape-stained linen of her sisters' garments, Milcah cherished the warmth, and the whispers, and the slightest scent of myrtle. What a blessing from God to be counted among the daughters of Zelophehad.

She glimpsed the road leading toward Megiddo.

No foe, nor chariot, nor beast tarried there.

29

When her older sisters had returned to their homes, Eli's donkey charged into the clearing braying its displeasure with his haste. Eli's expression did not hold the excitement of a bridegroom. He dismounted and stalked toward her.

For a brief moment, she considered racing into a nearby tent or running into the fields and hiding among the grape plants. She doubted his urgency was from fleeing stubborn goats.

Clasping her hands, she held them in front of her chest. "Did the livestock behave this morn?"

No answer came forth. If he had been one of her sisters, a multitude of words would have been spilled by now.

Eli crossed his arms and stroked his jaw as if discerning which rebuke to utter first. He didn't even peek inside the press to gauge the level of juice.

Should she speak about the pagan in earnest? How had gossip about her sisters managed to spread faster than butter on a baking stone?

Tirzah, who was bent over in the melon patch,

straightened and raced into the vineyard.

Coward.

Milcah met Eli's one-eyed stare and forced a smile. Better to confess outright than to allow suspicion to abound.

"My sisters and I stomped the grapes." Her sisters, less Hoglah, mashed grapes easily using their rage against the pagan. "We are hard workers."

Eli quirked a bushy brow. "They threaten fighting men as well. Barefoot."

"A fighting man," she offered. "There was only one. I believe you know of whom I speak?"

"I do."

The brevity of his answer caused her stomach to hollow.

"I believe he is gone for good this time." *Lord, may it be so.*

"A group of women scared him off." Eli's tone held a hint of jest. "Your sisters accomplished what the men of Manasseh could not?"

She rubbed her temples. How was a wife supposed to handle an upset husband? She was too young when her mother died to know.

"Perhaps the Canaanite will understand the relationship we have with the One True God. Even the pagans in the field sided with us."

Eli glanced at the newly arrived workers sitting near the press.

"Walk with me." He motioned for her to stroll along the hill. No one carted wine to the storehouse. Not yet.

"You're angry at me?" Her heart thumped louder than her sandal steps.

"More so at your sisters. I don't want harm to come to you."

Laughter broke free from her lips. "How my life has changed. Wasn't the gossip that I would bury a third man?"

"I do not believe you are cursed."

"No, you didn't." She grazed a hand over the grassy hill. "I was the meek sister."

Now it was her intended's time to laugh. "You? Meek?"

Eli led her around the slope of the hill and away from curious eyes. Years before, men must have removed some of the hill's dirt when the path to the well was forged. The slant was flatter here than in the front. She rested her back against the side of the mound. Grass soothed her tense muscles.

Eli picked at a turf of grass. "We need workers to help care for this vineyard. Our clansmen have helped us with the harvest, but if the elders begin to cast insults on my name, men may demand payment and quit their labors." Eli's shoulders slumped forward. "I have very little left to offer them."

Should she offer her means? "I could sell some of father's livestock."

Eli shook his wild mane of hair. "I won't allow it. We have to have some animals left to breed." He pounded the side of the hill, not in anger or in a threatening manner, but as a man bound to become more than people believed possible.

Their gazes met. The determination in his eye could have set her hair ablaze.

Maybe it was the discovery of Hoglah being with child. Or maybe it was the whispers of wedding tents. Or maybe it was Eli being so close and the breeze so delightful. Her flesh tingled.

Eli was here, and near, and…

She rocked forward to leave, to place a respectable distance between their bodies. They needed to part. Her sandal pushed hard against the hill.

And her foot kept moving. The hill was moving, shifting inward.

She was falling again. So was Eli.

Backward.

But still together.

30

Milcah's spine slammed into the dirt. Why was she lying flat inside of a hill? She didn't know how Eli managed to jerk sideways, so he didn't smash her into the ground, but he hit the dirt a few feet away.

Air, thick with dust, settled in her throat. Over and over, she coughed, gagging at the earthy grit in her mouth. Rolling onto her side, she braced herself against the floor. Of what? The stifling warmth and the aroma of soured grapes caused her stomach to heave. Settling in Canaan was more difficult than she had imagined.

Eli scrambled to his feet. He resembled a rabbit poking its head from an underground burrow. Clumps of earth, sod, and grass fell from his garment as he knelt beside her.

"Are you hurt?"

She sat, slowly. "I don't believe so." She tapped her sandals on the uneven ground trying to find level footing. Praise God. Her bones had hung together, but they protested the jolt from her fall. She swatted at a spider scurrying upward in its web. "Where are we?" Her gaze darted around the tomb-like space. Dark, water-stained beams supported the earthen ceiling above her as if the hill had a wooden rib cage. A domed wooden door had opened into the underbelly of the hill. Outside was the path they had trod. "Are we safe in here?"

Eli gripped her hand and pulled her upright. Surely, no one would protest his touch. He fanned the hazy air with his hands and inspected the structure above.

"The roof seems sound." He fixed his gaze on the length of the room. "I think we found what the pagan has been seeking: a secret storehouse for the king's wine."

"It's more like a burial chamber." She brushed off her skirt and followed Eli farther into the hill.

"If it was a burial chamber, we would smell the decay." He rubbed dirt from his nose and grimaced.

Jars, similar to the ones discovered in the main storehouse, filled the inside of the cave. Each vessel was emblazoned with a wax seal.

She ran her fingers over the cool clay of the jars. "This must be the king's mark?"

Eli chuckled. "We didn't go to the trouble of marking our harvest." He ventured farther into the shadows beneath the hill. He crouched and lifted something thin and long and curved and golden. "No wonder we were followed out of the city."

Gold. Her feet should have danced upon the clumps of displaced earth, but she couldn't forget her past. After Eli and Hoglah wandered into the pit at Peor, a plague came upon their camp. A fever almost killed her sister. Basemath had brought the image of a false god into her home on a golden armlet. Milcah shuddered.

"Is there an image on it?" She licked her lips. Her mouth tasted of mud. "If there is release it. You will die, Eli. You will die and everyone will blame me." With her frantic heartbeat, she could barely catch a breath. "Leave it be."

She had worked too hard harvesting her father's land and worked her sisters too hard for Eli to die and her land to be stolen away by the elders. She cared for Eli. Could she even cope with another loss? Slanderers would say Eli's blood was on her hands.

"Milcah." Eli's tone was as melodic as a harp. Had she ever heard him speak so softly? He held the gold lengthwise. "It's a ladle. There is no image etched into it. Come and see." He did not move. He waited for her to amble toward him.

Her hands stayed at her sides. She would not touch anything. Not until it had been deemed acceptable to God.

"Look. There is not a single etching." He continued to display the treasure. His eye glimmered brighter than the gold. "It seems the winemaker had a ladle for every jar. Do you know what this means?"

She still kept her distance. "We won't need to dip our wooden cups into the wine for a tasting?"

He laughed heartily. "We can pay our workers their wages."

"Praise God." She clasped her hands and lifted them toward the beams. "God has blessed us abundantly."

"He has indeed."

Resting the ladle in a crate lined with linen, Eli hoisted a bulky satchel. The clinks did not soothe her spirit. The embroidered cloth with hues of indigo and mustard was finer than any she had seen. A thick ribbon cinched the sack.

"Be careful," she cautioned. "The Canaanites have many gods." She clutched the top of a jar for balance.

Eli opened the sack and closed it straightaway. His rugged features drained of pleasure.

"These goblets hold the image of the goddess I chopped down near the well."

She backstepped toward the sunlight. "What will we do with them? Will you have to travel to Shiloh?" She did not desire for Eli to be gone for so many days.

Setting the satchel against the sloped wall of the cave, Eli nodded. "These need to be taken to the Levites and put into the Tabernacle treasury. Reuben or another elder can accompany me." He fisted the hand that held the sack. "The trip will not be quick, but the Levites must decide what is to be done with the gold." He brushed off his hands as he came closer. "Jericho was full of such spoils. As long as it is dedicated to God, no harm will come to us."

His words gave her some comfort.

"And what about the wine? Can we sell it—"

"Or use it?"

Her jaw clamped tight. Was Eli going to imbibe to excess? With all this wine, he could drink his fill and more.

"We do have a wedding celebration coming soon enough. As does your sister." Eli grinned and drew near. "Our guests will expect wine. More so now that we own a vineyard. The jars do not bear the image of a false god."

She nibbled her lip. Would Tirzah or Enid object to the wine?

"The same grapes that we crushed also produced this drink," Eli said. His words were void of any encouragement or discouragement.

Her nostrils itched from all the disrupted dust. She scratched her nose and sniffed.

"We will serve it only if Mahlah and the elders agree it is acceptable. I do not want any gossiping going on while I'm in my wedding tent."

Eli stifled a grin and nodded. "I don't want you wasting time listening for slander when we are finally together."

Cheeks growing hotter, she cleared her throat and said nothing. What does one say to a bridegroom concerning his wedding tent?

"Milcah." Her name sounded from the path.

Truly her sister would be concerned about her absence. Lamech's aunt may have sent her to find them.

"Sister?" Tirzah's summons filled with angst.

Milcah hurried toward the opening in the hill and dodged clumps of displaced dirt. She shaded her eyes from the brightness.

"Tirzah. I'm here."

Her sister hunched by the fallen sod on the path. "Praise God. I thought you had been crushed by a landslide."

Emerging from the king's secret storehouse, Milcah embraced her sister. "Come inside and see what we found. Inside this hill are jars of the king's wine and some golden dippers."

"Gold?" Tirzah's eyes grew as wide as the opening. "Perhaps I shouldn't have traded my portion of land."

"Most of the wealth will go the Levites," Eli said as he stomped over debris. "And to Lamech and Enid's cousins. The wine can be served at our celebration."

"We must tell Enid." Tirzah bounced on her sandals. "He will be relieved that he does not have to sell some of his livestock."

Milcah turned and beheld the strange storehouse. God had provided a means to pay their kinsmen. She and Eli did not have to sell any of her father's livestock or be indebted to her sisters' husbands. *Toda raba, Adonai.*

Inside her heart, a lily bloomed. No one could say she was cursed. A tear streamed down her cheek, but she swept it away. She was not unhappy. She was thankful and blessed. God had bestowed on her and Eli the king's vineyard, his golden ladles, and his wine aplenty. She hoped, maybe, just maybe, her people would forget her past woes and the rumors of a curse, and that they would praise the blessing of her inheritance.

~*~

The following afternoon, Eli, Reuben, and a few clansmen set out with the satchel of forbidden spoils to deliver the wealth to Shiloh, to their leader Joshua, and to the Levites. They also placed a few jars of royal wine in the wagon for the Tabernacle servants.

Lamech's cousins had gladly accepted the golden ladles as payment for their labors in the fields and on the treading floor. And since so many jars rested under the hill, she and Eli had a few ladles of their own.

When evening fell and she returned to her tent, she found a small pouch lying on her bed mat. She grasped the burlap and instantly knew what was inside by the size, by the smooth feel, and by the tiny rough nodule at the top of the loop. And she knew Eli had slipped into her tent and delivered this gift. Opening the pouch, she let the ring fall into her palm. Her chest sagged at the sight of the familiar gold band with the handsome cut ruby. Her treasure held the memory of Hanoch. While her heart remembered her former intended, it did not pain her as much. As much as it had when she received the news of his death. A love for Eli had started to take root in the hidden places of her heart where her memories were stored. She had a new intended now, and her fondness for him had begun to flourish.

She had reasons to rejoice and not to mourn.

As tears filled her eyes, she whispered, "Toda raba, Adonai."

31

With the harvest over, and Eli on his way to Shiloh with Reuben, Mahlah insisted Milcah and Tirzah gather on her land in order to prepare for the upcoming wedding celebrations. Upon Mahlah's announcement, Lamech's aunt whipped her donkey into a trot and fled the vineyard.

Milcah packed the back of a cart with melons from her sprawling patch. She grasped a thick prickly stem and sawed back and forth with the gift Eli had given her. A blade did make a useful present after all.

A bead of sweat slid along her head covering and slithered into her eye. The sting clouded her vison. She halted her knife's work.

"Are you leaving us?" Yarrat approached. He advanced ahead of his mother who strolled slowly with Doti.

Blinking, Milcah glanced at the boy and rose. "Only for a while. For enough time to marry Eli." She swept a hand across her forehead.

"Why aren't you wearing your ruby ring?" Yarrat asked, eyes intent on her hands.

"Yarrat," his mother cautioned.

Milcah stared at her bare fingers. "How did you know about my ring?" The boy did seem to know everything, but Eli had only recently returned it to her tent.

Yarrat crossed his arms and broadened his slim chest. "I went with Eli into the city."

"You did?" Her mind wandered to the image of the pagan stomping on Yarrat's belly. "Weren't you afraid of seeing the warrior again?"

"Not now. Now that I serve the One True God." Yarrat stretched to his full height. "We did not see that man or his chariot."

"Truly?" Her voice rushed forth as her spirit took flight. "The warrior was not in the city? And you believe in our God?"

Zhirta hurried forward and dipped her head. "We have never seen women stand in front of an armed fighter and speak so boldly. Your God must be strong. We want to be strong, too."

Milcah matched the mother's toothy smile. "Our God is the God of the orphan and the widow. God has blessed my sisters. We were doing what our leader Joshua commanded. To be strong and courageous." She shifted toward Yarrat. "And you will need to be strong and courageous, Yarrat, for there is a sign of God's covenant worn by our men. Usually, it is done on the eighth day after a son is born, but you are much older."

"I know." Yarrat's nose crinkled. "Eli mentioned it to me. He said I would hurt for a few days."

Toda raba, Eli, for explaining circumcision. Now, she wouldn't have to discuss the removal of a foreskin as a sign of God's covenant.

"We will do what the One True God requires of us." Zhirta lifted Doti and settled the young girl on her hip. "If we serve the Hebrew God, will we be able to live on His land?"

Milcah swept a dark curl from Doti's eye lashes. She wanted the widow and her children to be safe, but she could not make that decision. "After you meet with the elders and Yarrat is healed, then we will discuss a place for you to live." Hands on her hips, she surveyed the rows of grape plants covering the fields. "Yarrat, you seem to know this vineyard better than anyone. Is there open land where we could build homes? Not too far from the clearing but far enough from the noise of the workers?"

The boy nodded in earnest. "I will show you when Eli returns. There is a spot where you can see the slope of the hill and no one will see you."

"Good." So Eli had mentioned the king's wine. Knowing Yarrat, he would have found out soon enough. "We will also need harvesters again. You can help us tend the vineyard."

Zhirta's cheeks flooded with tears. "You are too generous. Praise God."

Milcah startled. Hadn't she and her sisters been saying that very phrase for years. All of their lives.

"Pay guh," Doti mumbled.

"You are learning already young one." She laughed at the girl's enthusiasm. "I cannot wait to sing the praises of my…our God, to you."

But first, she had a wedding celebration to attend.

32

Many days later, after Eli had returned from Shiloh, Milcah slid forward on her bed mat. The reeds in the weave were as slick as olive oil for all the years she had reclined on the thin cushion. She faced inward, toward a circle of her sisters. Tomorrow, this very tent would be where she and Eli truly became husband and wife. Some clansmen had already arrived for the celebration and were staking their temporary dwellings on Reuben's and Mahlah's vast inheritance. But tonight, Milcah was with her family, her sisters, in a tent of women nestled farther from the road and away from curious eyes. Mahlah's land held many grand trees to shield her sisters.

Out of the way, bundled in a blanket, Miriam, Aaron, and Abigail slept peacefully in the tent. By the next harvest, Hoglah would have her own babe, and the nest of young children would grow larger. Maybe even with her own child. A stream of energy surged through her veins at the thought of birthing an heir.

"Hand me a bowl," Hoglah whispered. "My stomach settles at night, but I do not want to take any chances."

Milcah offered Hoglah a large serving bowl.

"Wait." Tirzah grabbed Milcah's wrist and held it so the ruby glistened in the lamplight. "Why didn't I notice this before? You're wearing Hanoch's ring. Did you buy it back from the merchant?"

"What merchant?" Mahlah rose on her forearms. "You wouldn't sell such a gift?"

Fumbling for an explanation, Milcah wrapped a strand of hair around her finger. With her nieces and nephews asleep, she could not hope for an interruption.

"I bartered my ring so Eli and I would have jars for our wine." There, she had acknowledged her sacrifice. "I didn't want to be a burden on my family. Any more than I have been with the harvest." Sitting, she faced Tirzah. "Eli bought the ring from the merchant with the wealth we found in the hill. Yarrat told me so. I found the band in a pouch on my bed mat."

"Why would you sell the ruby?" Noah shifted closer. "I could have given you livestock."

Milcah shook her head. "Our livestock will breed and support our future. A ring cannot. Truly, you need not be concerned, the ring has been returned."

Mahlah bobbed her head. "You have always been wise beyond your years, Sister."

Hoglah pinched Milcah's chin. "This is the same Eli who chopped down the idol. Perhaps he is taking some of our sister's wisdom to heart?"

"That," — Noah laughed as though she held a secret — "and my husband held him by the neck after his fall from the tree. We made sure he knew not to dishonor our good name."

Mahlah rolled over, laughing. "Now, I have heard it all. Our name has been the spark of more gossip than any other name. I am pleased Eli hasn't added more kindling to the blaze. From what I have witnessed in this valley, he has worked hard and made wise decisions." Mahlah tilted her head. "Such as buying your ring from the barterer."

A long-winded breath filled the intimate circle. Tirzah slung an arm over Milcah's shoulder. "Eli is marrying Milcah. How could he not succeed?"

"Toda raba, Sister." Milcah breathed in the soft scent of myrtle and campfire smoke trapped in Tirzah's hair. "Tomorrow, I may shed a tear that we are not sharing a tent. We have been together the longest."

"Ugh. Don't make me cry. Our lands still border each other." Tirzah kissed Milcah on the cheek. "And you have a well for watering our livestock." Tirzah quirked an eyebrow. "But Enid has been most patient. If I do not show at this ceremony on the morrow, he will storm this tent, as Reuben did for Mahlah, and kiss me most thoroughly."

Mahlah pounded her finger against the nearest mat. "You did not listen to me. When Reuben entered our tent to seek my hand, I told you all to face the side of the tent."

"We did face away," Noah said. "For a moment. Then we peeked to see what all the fuss was about."

"Reuben wasn't fussing." Hoglah scooted closer to the center of the circle. "He needed air. Mahlah clutched him tight with all ten fingernails." Hoglah puckered her lips and made kissing noises.

Hushed laughter rippled through the tent.

Milcah cherished her sisters' banter. Inside, her belly felt like a jumble of smooth ribbons. She hadn't kissed a man on the lips. Yet.

"How will I know how to kiss Eli?"

"Yes, tell us." Tirzah seemed eager to listen for once.

Hoglah held her arms high and then pressed her palms together. "When you're this close, tilt your head toward your husband and then..." Hoglah's eyes grew wide as her gaze swept around the circle. "And then stop talking."

"Remember to breathe," Noah added. "Or you'll faint and miss your first night."

"Shhh." Tirzah cupped a hand to her ear. "I hear someone outside of the tent. What if it's Keenan?"

Mahlah's brow furrowed. "I set the wedding tents far from the tables and the cooking pit. Guests should not be wandering among the trees." Mahlah shifted closer to the tent flap. "Keenan and his wife staked a tent near the feasting tables. I doubt he is listening. His schemes to acquire our land have failed."

Lounging on her side, Noah finger brushed her wavy hair. "Jeremiah will keep watch over his brother. Milcah and Eli will be in this very tent by sundown."

Milcah shivered. She cared for Eli. She desired to be his wife. But being a wife was something she knew very little about. And time spent with Eli was time spent away from her sisters. Tears warmed her eyes.

"I'm going to miss our tent talks."

Tears slipped from Tirzah's eyes. "Me, as well."

"Oh, now." Mahlah sniffled and knelt in the center of their bed mat circle. She embraced the youngest daughters of Zelophehad. "We shall do this again. I will make sure of it. We go forth with God, but we also go forth with each other. That will never change."

"Ever." Noah joined and comforted her sisters.

Hoglah crouched by the tent flap, delicately unlacing the ties. She wrenched the ramskin apart and poked her head outside of the tent.

Was her sister ill?

"Aha! Tirzah was correct." Hoglah vanished and returned with Basemath and a fist full of their former neighbor's robe.

Reuben's sister crossed her arms as if she had every

right to linger and listen. "You whisper loudly. You always have."

Silence.

Milcah met her sisters' gazes. Should they invite Basemath into their tent?

Hoglah pulled Basemath toward the intimate circle. "You can stay and whisper with us. Though, you can't go into labor, or we will push you from the tent. We don't have time to birth a baby. We are celebrating our youngest sisters tomorrow."

Milcah tucked Hoglah's sentiment into her heart. After spending a night with her sisters, she could face anything, by going forth with God and her God-fearing sisters.

Basemath wedged between Mahlah and Hoglah. her lips were pressed thin and her eyes glistened. When she was settled, she said, "I want to be a daughter of Zelophehad."

More silence. Then everyone laughed.

Who wouldn't want the blessing of sisters?

And God had blessed her with an abundance.

33

Milcah's fingers trembled as she reached for one of Hoglah's raisin cakes. Overhead, the sun warmed the shriveled grapes and cast a festive glare on the oakwood feasting tables. Eli lounged at the far end of the table. Hair banded neatly and dressed in an embroidered alabaster-hued robe, her husband appeared elegant and worthy of all the gold they had found in the hill. Jeremiah made sure his brother's cup brimmed with goat's milk or fresh water.

Praise of the king's wine rippled through her clansmen's chatter. She prayed all the effort these past weeks would bring about acceptable wine next year.

As she turned to admire Tirzah bathed in the shade of a grand oak, the tiny polished-bronzed beads attached to Milcah's headband *tinked* softly. Mahlah had insisted Milcah wear the tiny trinkets, since they resembled grape clusters. Her nephews, Daniel and Jonah, had found colored stones to adorn Tirzah's band.

Enid feasted on roasted lamb with his brothers. Lamech had held several cups of the king's wine high in celebration of his younger brother. Somehow, in her memory, Enid would always be the shepherd boy who tagged along with her and Tirzah in the outskirts of Gilgal. The boy had grown into a capable keeper of livestock.

Noah approached with baby Miriam resting comfortably against her chest. Wide-eyed and chubby-cheeked, Milcah's niece brought visions of Doti crawling through the grape plants.

"You must eat something." Noah shimmered in the sunlight. Silver stars, strung across her forehead, caught the sun's rays and cast moving bursts of light on the wooden table. "Your melon is ripe and Hoglah's roasted lamb has never tasted better. She even spiced my goat cheese."

Milcah's stomach hurt as if she had feasted like a glutton. "I will try to eat, but hunger is the least of my worries." She leaned closer to her sister. "When this day is over, I pray no one will speak of a curse. Men should be remembered for their sacrifice, not because of their affection for me."

Noah glanced at her in-laws reclining at a nearby table. "We all know who disperses slander." She shifted her precious daughter. "Men die in war, and we know how much war we have endured. Anyone blaming you for the deaths of two fighting men is a fool."

Milcah reached for Noah's hand. "Toda raba," she said softly, and swallowed the lump forming in her throat. "Now that we are settled, may we not have to fight many wars. I believe mother and father would be proud at our hospitality and how we have shared our blessings with our clan."

Warm and calloused, Noah's hand stroked away some of Milcah's fears.

"God watched over us when we marched in the desert, tended livestock in the fields, staked our tents in camp; and now, he watches over us in this valley." Noah kissed Milcah's temple. Miriam tried unsuccessfully to capture the glistening cluster-like beads with her tiny fingers. "My quiet sister manages the king's vineyard. God is truly faithful."

Clap. Stomp. Clap.

Lamech pounded a rhythm with his sandals. His laughter drowned out the melodic music from their kinsmen plucking stringed lyres.

"My brother and his bride will fill many tents with their offspring." Lamech whirled in a circle. After steadying himself, he said, "My wife and I will fill a tent soon enough."

Hoglah hurried toward her husband with a platter of roasted meat in hand.

"I must see to my in-laws." Noah nodded toward Abishua, his wife Peninnah, and Keenan dining at a nearby table. "Keenan can fetch his own drink." Noah leaned close and whispered.

Milcah dipped her head. How much longer did she need to stay? She shouldn't be expected to linger at the table. Her kinsmen would understand her rush to her wedding tent.

Enid rose from his shaded seat of honor despite Tirzah's attempts to keep him seated.

"Beautiful are the daughters of Zelophehad." Enid joined his brother. Arm in arm, they bounded around in a dance, spinning faster and faster.

Mahlah and Reuben sauntered closer to the raucous action.

Enid pointed at Milcah's table.

Oh, no, no, no. Her intended did not need to dance. Though, perhaps she could whisk Eli away if he got to his feet.

"Do you not agree, my brother? To the beauty of our

wives?" Enid grinned at Tirzah who had a melon ball in her hand. Would she eat it or toss it?

Praise be. Tirzah chewed the fruit madly.

Eli glanced Milcah's way, his dark eye fiery in the sunlight. Clear of focus among the commotion of their guests, he beheld her with admiration.

At that moment, she forgot the pain of loss. The long months of mourning. She simply basked in Eli's devotion and God's blessing. She had her land, her sisters, and a husband.

"My wife is a blossom of beauty," Eli called out. He pushed back from the table and rose. Eli joined Lamech and Enid under the branches of the oak.

She remembered the lily she had burned. Oh, if only she had a centerpiece of lilies on her table.

Stomp. Clap. Stomp.

Eli lifted his arms and danced like a giddy bridegroom.

What a blessing to see her husband carefree and happy. *Clap. Clap. Clap.* She encouraged his joyous footfalls.

His family joined in the merriment, clapping a bit less enthusiastically. Jeremiah, big and rugged, joined with his brother parading round and round in a circle.

The gathering of kin widened, giving Eli room to show his gratefulness to God in a dance.

She sputtered a laugh. She had never seen Eli celebrating his blessings after his injury. This perfect moment, she would treasure. Eli leaping. Eli flailing.

Eli?

Rushing sounds like a gust of wind filled the space under the oak branches. But it wasn't air moving. Dirt moved, vanishing from sight as if the earth called it home.

"Eli," she shrieked.

Her husband was nowhere to be seen. Her heart skittered in her chest as she kicked back her chair. An odd, eerie hum deafened her cries. *Not again. Please God, not again.*

She raced toward where Eli had danced. Toward a hole in the ground void of soil, or rock, or earth. This opening had swallowed another intended. It had swallowed another love.

Kinsmen scattered away from the opening.

Mahlah gasped. "My children were playing there this morn."

Lyre strumming stopped. Wailing and shrieks shattered the festivities.

Milcah bit her lip. Blood, not the taste of raisin cakes, settled on her tongue as she neared where she had last seen Eli frolicking.

Where was her husband?

34

Milcah dropped to her knees and crawled nearer the opening in the ground, but not too near. She didn't want to fall into the hole or send anymore dirt and debris cascading onto Eli. She was determined to save her bridegroom and save her land.

"Eli," she summoned again and again.

No answer came forth.

"Remove her," someone yelled. "She wants to bury him."

Mahlah and Reuben crouched on either side of her. They consoled her with a jumble of words her ears failed to comprehend. Did they believe another body would be buried in Canaan? Another man who had sung his admiration of her would be lamented and mourned?

Staring at the opening, blinking at the haze of dust rising into the air, she prayed, short and sure. *Lord, save Eli from the dark pit.* She knew she wasn't cursed. How could a daughter of the Most High God carry a curse? God would not take her love when she was hours away from entering a wedding tent.

She was mostly sure of her petition. The uncertainty caused her stomach to heave.

"We have to get Eli out of the hole." Her words held a hint of hope as she beheld Reuben and Mahlah. "We must raise him out of the opening."

Mahlah and Reuben exchanged a look of helplessness. Their mouths hung open, but they did not affirm her request. When had Milcah ever seen her eldest sister so still amidst a commotion?

Standing at a safe distance from the collapsed earth, on the other side of the hole, Keenan jabbed a finger in the direction of her face.

"That woman killed my brother. She is responsible for his death. Her land will be a burial ground lest we act."

"Untrue." Mahlah sprang to her feet. "My sister wasn't even dancing near your brother."

Noah pushed through the mass of guests staring slack-jawed at the ground. "Do you not have eyes to see?" Noah indicated the opening. "Your brother fell into an old well or a pagan's trap. Do not cast blame on my sister. Anyone could have fallen through the dirt. Why don't you inspect the drop and see if your brother lives?"

"And risk my life? Send your sister. She will fit into the well." Keenan nodded toward the elders present. "What will she have to live for if another husband perishes?"

How dare that schemer cast doubt on her future. She

had to believe God would spare Eli, but not if everyone kept talking and lounging by the hole.

Jeremiah blocked an angry Noah from circling the opening and confronting Keenan.

Seizing the diversion, she slid on her belly closer to the opening. Earth warmed her skin as tiny pebbles embedded in her palms. Closer and closer, she inched. The *tink* of her polished bronze clusters was all she heard. Halting at the edge, she peeked into the deep crevice. Loose dirt crumbled into the abyss where the sun's rays did not reach.

Her heart developed wings as she glimpsed the top of Eli's head. His hair, or what resembled his mane, blended in with the shadows and the soil.

"Eli, I'm here."

She strained her neck to see if Eli moved or breathed or anything. A rock loosened and plummeted onto Eli's head.

"She's burying him alive," Keenan shouted.

Fool.

A sputtering cough rumbled from the pit.

God, please. Spare my Eli.

"Eli, I'm up here. Say something to your bride." Could she hear a reply with her heart thundering in her ears?

She waited. Waited on God.

"Milcah?" Eli's response was as delicate as a sun-scorched shell.

Praise be! "Don't move. You've fallen in a well. I'm coming to get you."

"I can't…move."

"Don't try. I don't want you to fall farther."

"Make haste." Eli's voice was but a breath. "There's nothing below my feet."

Turning her head to the side, she called to her sisters.

"Gather rope and tie it to my ankles." She licked her lips, but they dried instantly. "Your husbands can lower me down and pull Eli and me out of the pit."

Lamech came forward. "I have rope."

"I'll tie it," Noah said. "If you touch her legs, the elders will chastise us again."

Mahlah grabbed a coil. "I will help. Forgive me sister, for this will be tight."

"Do not worry about my ankles. If the earth quakes, I will lose my husband."

Tirzah and Hoglah hurried over with a cloth from the feasting tables.

"We will cover her legs, so no one sees any flesh." Hoglah fanned the linen as if she was dressing a table.

A slight breeze cooled Milcah's body before the drape of cloth weighted her legs. Blood pulsed in her ankles where the ropes dug into her flesh. She flung her head covering and tinkling headband off to the side of the opening.

Prone on the ground, she lifted onto her elbows and crawled forward until she pitched downward. Tension on her legs kept her from falling fast. Head first and hands outstretched, she descended into the hole. Stuffy air clogged her nostrils. She willed herself not to cough. The gasps and mutterings of her wedding guests sounded as if they were overcome by dust as well.

Hanging by her feet, she called out, "Lower." She used enough force in her command without startling the earth. Her temples grew warm and thudded their disapproval at her upside-down position.

Sunlight from above showed Eli wedged in the circular pit, arms at his sides.

When her fingertips touched Eli's coarse mane of hair, she yelled for her brothers-in-law to stop lowering her body. Too much rope and her weight may dislodge her husband. What lay beneath them was a mystery she did not want to solve. Good thing she was the slightest sister.

Between Eli's arms and his chest, she burrowed her hands. "Do not laugh," she whispered. "We will have to run to our wedding tent after my wanton touching."

His agreement hummed in his throat and vibrated across her chest.

She wiggled her fingers until they passed through the warmth of Eli's body and scraped the side of the pit. Hardened dirt clawed at her knuckles while the sting of raw flesh burned the top of her hands. She flexed her fingers to lace them tight around her husband.

Hanoch's ring snagged on the side of the pit. It slipped like silk down her finger. She tried to curve her fingertip, but it was gone. What could she do? She hung from a rope, cheek to cheek with Eli, their bodies breathing as one. She couldn't compare the loss of his life to the loss of a gold band. Hadn't God given her and Eli a hill full of gold?

Strangely, the place in her heart where she stored memories of Hanoch didn't pull or pinch. Her heart continued to beat normally. As normally as one suspended in a pit beneath the ground.

"Something hit my leg," Eli mumbled.

"Perhaps a rock loosened." A ruby rock. She would tell him what happened someday, but not today.

"I love you, Milcah." Eli's confession tickled her ear.

"You are saying that because you are in my grasp."

"I will shout it when I am confident it won't bury us." His head turned slightly ever closer. The bristle of his jaw sent a flutter through her body. "I loved you when you did not wail when you were bound to me. I wanted to make you proud. God blessed me with you and now we are in a pit."

She tightened her hold. "We are getting out of this pit. Together. Like we harvested our vineyard." She pressed her cheek closer, against the smooth leather of his eye patch. "Forgive me for not understanding what life was like for you. I was my father's fourth daughter, and I believe I received more love and acceptance than you."

"From your sisters?"

"Yes. I have the best sisters. And my parents."

"You are the best sister."

"Don't say that too loud for my sisters' husbands are holding the rope."

"One is my brother." Eli grunted and struggled to breathe.

"I am very fond of Jeremiah."

"So am I. That may be the first time I have spoken his praise. I will have to tell him so."

She secured her hold. "Let's go up into the light, husband." Turning from Eli's ear, she shouted, "Lift us out of this pit."

35

Maintaining a fierce grip around Eli's chest, Milcah ascended. She felt for the edge of the pit with the tips of her sandals. Rough, baked earth was not kind to her toes or her shins. Her dutiful sisters clothed her naked legs as her brothers-in-law drew her from the opening. The daughters of Zelophehad didn't need any more scandals on this celebratory day.

As soon as Eli was pulled safely from the pit, the string players plucked their lyres in earnest. How easily the celebration resumed.

"My son is alive." Abishua rushed toward Eli who sat, hunched, a safe distance from the hole.

Milcah's husband removed rubble and dirt from his robe.

Eli's mother, Peninnah, wept loudly, louder than when her son vanished beneath the ground.

"Are you hurt?" Mahlah's long hair tickled Milcah's skin as her oldest sister inspected every scratch. "We must wash these legs."

Milcah swallowed the grit in her throat. "I am well, Sister."

"You mean you fell in one." Noah winked and embraced her with abandon.

Hugs. Touching. Tears. Her sisters' hands stroked Milcah's arms and legs. Her husband did not come from a family that cherished every member. That would have to change. She could not remember a day that she had not been smothered with love by her sisters. How blessed she had been and remained.

Near the feasting tables, elders toasted Eli's rescue with the king's wine. A tongue lashing did not seem forthcoming about her curse.

Milcah removed herself from the bustle of her sisters and stood. Had hanging upside down made her taller than Tirzah? Her younger sister bounced on tiptoe trying to replace Milcah's head covering and bronze-clustered headband.

"We will never forget our wedding celebration." Tirzah swept wetness from her eyes and smiled her mischievous, youngest-sister smile.

"Why should we give the gossipers a rest?" Milcah laughed and embraced Tirzah. She even embraced Basemath and her belly.

Eli scuffled with his brothers. "I'm fine." His voice boomed over the festivities. "Bring some cleansing jars to my tent. Hurry now."

Her husband shuffled closer and shooed away her sisters with a wave of his hand.

"You're covered with dirt," Hoglah said, barely giving Eli a foothold. "You need a bath as does my sister."

"You speak the truth." Eli bent, and before Milcah knew what was happening, one strong arm wrapped around her back and the other lifted her off of her feet.

Mahlah followed after her as Eli headed toward the tables. "Where are you taking my sister."

"Where she belongs. To our wedding tent." Eli's announcement quieted the crowd. "We can bathe each other."

"Eli." She lowered her voice. "Such talk is scandalous."

"I'm not taking any chances." Eli slowed his jog toward the wedding tents. "I don't want to fall again or be part of any other woe."

"Ah." Tirzah whined, flailing her arms. "I'm last again."

"Shalom, clan of Hepher," Eli yelled as he dipped under the tent flap.

Milcah's insides were all a jumble, but not because of her bridegroom's bumpy carry. Tonight, she would share a bed with her husband. A husband she had grown to love. She had prayed to God for a betrothal, and He had answered her petition His way. *Praise be to the One True God.*

Eli settled her carefully onto her feet. His hands cradled her face as his gaze beheld her like a royal beauty.

When he drew close to kiss her, she remembered Hoglah's wisdom.

She tilted her head and stopped talking.

A Devotional Moment

Joshua said to them, "Do not be afraid; do not be discouraged. Be strong and courageous. This is what the Lord will do to all the enemies you are going to fight."
~ Joshua 10:25

God promises to go into battle with us always. Whether it is a war of the flesh, heart, or mind, He is a constant companion in our time of need. When we accept God as our Saviour, we step into a battle for our souls. Temptations will abound, things of the fallen world will be tossed in our path to make us stumble or fall. But God is our rock, our steadfast defender, and He promises to help us over every obstacle, large or small.

In **Claiming Canaan: Milcah's Journey**, the protagonist has lost too much several times. The culture of the day requires that she conform or lose all that she holds dear. In a battle of wills, she must persevere to hold on to her God-given rights.

Have you ever felt torn between doing what your peers want and doing what you know to be right? It can be difficult to face rejection or ridicule or loss, but your strength of character comes directly from God. All you have to do is let it shine through. When you stand with courage and strength, God upholds you through every battle to the end. He tells you in His Word that all things will pass. And it always does. This life is impermanent, but God's Kingdom is everlasting. Hold on and face whatever life throws at you. God has your back.

LORD, WHEN I AM WEAK, HELP ME TO BE STRONG AND COURAGEOUS AND TO FACE ALL BATTLES WITH YOUR GRACE. IN JESUS' NAME I PRAY, AMEN.

A Note from Barbara

Thank you for continuing on my journey with the daughters of Zelophehad. I couldn't leave these girls without having them settle their land.

The beginning crisis in *Claiming Canaan* has Milcah fighting to save her portion of land. In Joshua 17:3-4, we are told the daughters went to Joshua to remind him about their inheritance. We don't know why they felt the need to remind Joshua about their portion of land, but it had been over seven years since Moses told the leaders of Israel about God's declaration. I have made Milcah's unmarried status a problem for the elders of the tribe of Manasseh. Was she married by now? We are never told who the daughters married or when they married.

We also don't know exactly where the daughters' land was located. I looked at the land bestowed on the tribe of Manasseh and placed the daughters in a perilous place—near Canaanite cities that had lost their kings but still housed idol worshipers. I placed the daughters near Megiddo.

Meggido is mentioned in Deborah's song in Judges 5:19, but it is also where the last battle of Armageddon will be fought (Revelation 16:16). I decided to put the descendants of faith-filled women in a place where the ultimate spiritual battle will be waged. Perhaps you know who I had in mind as the mysterious warrior Milcah faces outside of Megiddo.

Why did I bestow a vineyard on Milcah and Eli? In I Kings 21, we see a vineyard in Jezreel owned by Naboth. Naboth would not sell his vineyard to the king because his land was an inheritance from God. Naboth's allegiance to God's law cost him his life. We also see that the industrious and noble "Proverbs 31 Woman" planted a vineyard out of her earnings (Proverbs 31:16). A vineyard is a beautiful setting to show God's Creation, His blessings, and His abundance in harvest. And Hoglah needed raisins to make her delicious cakes.

God's Word never ceases to inspire me. That is why I enjoy bringing little-known Bible stories to light. I hope the daughters of Zelophehad encourage you to be strong and courageous in the Lord, and to go forth with God.

May the Lord bless you and keep you.

You Can Help!

At Pelican Book Group it is our mission to entertain readers with fiction that uplifts the Gospel. It is our privilege to spend time with you awhile as you read our stories.

We believe you can help us to bring Christ into the lives of people across the globe. And you don't have to open your wallet or even leave your house!

Here are 3 simple things you can do to help us bring illuminating fiction™ to people everywhere.

1) If you enjoyed this book, write a positive review. Post it at online retailers and websites where readers gather. And share your review with us at reviews@pelicanbookgroup.com (this does give us permission to reprint your review in whole or in part.)

2) If you enjoyed this book, recommend it to a friend in person, at a book club or on social media.

3) If you have suggestions on how we can improve or expand our selection, let us know. We value your opinion. Use the contact form on our web site or e-mail us at customer@pelicanbookgroup.com

God Can Help!

Are you in need? The Almighty can do great things for you. Holy is His Name! He has mercy in every generation. He can lift up the lowly and accomplish all things. Reach out today.

Do not fear: I am with you; do not be anxious: I am your God. I will strengthen you, I will help you, I will uphold you with my victorious right hand.

~Isaiah 41:10 (NAB)

We pray daily, and we especially pray for everyone connected to Pelican Book Group—that includes you! If you have a specific need, we welcome the opportunity to pray for you. Share your needs or praise reports at http://pelink.us/pray4us

Free eBook Offer

We're looking for booklovers like you to partner with us!
Join our team of influencers today and periodically receive
free eBooks!

For more information
Visit http://pelicanbookgroup.com/booklovers

How About Free Audiobooks?

We're looking for audiobook lovers, too! Partner with us
as an audiobook lover and periodically receive free
audiobooks!

For more information
Visit
http://pelicanbookgroup.com/booklovers/freeaudio.html

or e-mail
booklovers@pelicanbookgroup.com

CPSIA information can be obtained
at www.ICGtesting.com
Printed in the USA
FSHW010504230420
69281FS